STEPHEN ORAM writes thought provoking stories that mix science fiction with social comment, mainly in a recognisable near-future. He is the Author in Residence at Virtual Futures, once described by *The Guardian* as 'the Glastonbury of cyberculture'. He's keen on collaborating with scientists and future-tech people to write short stories that provoke debate about potential futures; the title story, Eating Robots, came from working with the Human Brain Project and Bristol Robotics Laboratory.

As a teenager he was heavily influenced by the ethos of punk. In his early twenties he embraced the squatter scene and was part of a religious cult, briefly. He did some computer stuff in what became London's silicon roundabout and is now a civil servant with a gentle attraction to anarchism.

He has two published novels, *Quantum Confessions* and *Fluence*, and several shorter pieces.

Visit stephenoram.net
Twitter @OramStephen
Facebook Stephen Oram Author

NUDGE THE FUTURE VOL 1

EATING ROBOTS

AND OTHER STORIES

STEPHEN ORAM

SilverWood

Published in 2017 by SilverWood Books

SilverWood Books Ltd
14 Small Street, Bristol, BS1 1DE, United Kingdom
www.silverwoodbooks.co.uk

ISBN 978-1-78132-622-0 (paperback)
ISBN 978-1-78132-623-7 (ebook)

British Library Cataloguing in Publication Data
A CIP catalogue record for this book is available from the British Library

Page design and typesetting by SilverWood Books
Printed on responsibly sourced paper

In memory of my brother, Robert

CONTENTS

DISJOINTED

He stood naked in front of the full-length mirror, flexing his biceps.

The mirror flashed an amber warning, reminding him to stand still while it scanned his organs, blood, bones and skin. It would evaluate his health and adjust the multitude of enhancement implants scattered throughout his body, fine-tuning them as it went to maximise his physical and mental performance.

This daily routine made him feel trapped and cornered, as if the mirror was a docking bay that he couldn't stay away from for more than twenty-four hours. He wanted to run into the sea or drink himself silly. He wanted to go off-grid and wander wherever he liked and for as long as he liked.

The pressure to break free had been building for a while, to such an extent that he doubted whether he could make it through another day.

As the timer in the top right-hand corner approached zero, he tightened his stomach muscles and straightened his back. The mirror snapped its daily photo for his archives and, he suspected, a central database.

He clenched his fist and punched the mirror with all the force he could summon. A thousand pieces flew across the room. The holistic guardian of his well-being was dismembered and lying scattered all around him.

An enormous sense of relief welled up from deep inside.

But.

What was that?

The fragments of the mirror were continuing their work in isolation and different parts of his body were choosing their own settings.

His hands were getting warmer, his feet colder. His heart was racing. His stomach clenched and his calf muscles cramped. And yet as soon as his brain registered a problem, it told him not to worry, immediately overriding all warnings.

He screamed as the pain and euphoria of the dissection reached every part of his being.

LITTLE MODERN MIRACLES

A stone hit the side of Rory's head, followed by a lump of soil; soil that would kill if it found its way into the bloodstream. Traces of it stuck to his hot, clammy face.

The crowd shouted at him.

'Dirty man!'

'Filth!'

'Pus lover!'

One person started a chant and the rest picked it up quickly. 'Sepsis. Sepsis. Sepsis.'

He walked as fast as he could, although his shallow breathing made it difficult. He wiped his face clean with his sweat-drenched T-shirt and blinked rapidly, activating his contact lenses to display the status of his health. His heart rate was up and it was predicting liver failure. The crowd was right; he had septicaemia and maybe even sepsis. He checked his arm. The infected wound was getting worse. It was oozing pus and the web of lines on the surface of his skin was getting bigger.

He needed antibiotics if he was going to survive. His only hope was finding the illegal sellers he'd encountered a few days before.

The sound of a portable loudspeaker system was coming from the next street. He couldn't quite catch what was being said, but it definitely had the dramatic rhythm and flow of someone selling the dreams of false religion or illegal drugs.

He dragged himself towards the source of the salesman's promises.

The street opened up into a large market square where, sure enough, there was a truck with its tailgate lowered to form a make-shift stage. A man and a woman dressed in plain suits spouted their sales pitch from the tailgate. Large images of them were displayed on the side panels of the truck, which had been swivelled around to form screens on either side.

'It's the miracle they don't want you to have,' said the man in low soothing tones.

Rory stumbled and swallowed the bile that had erupted at the sight of the couple. Seeing them in action again made him angry. He checked inside his pocket. Yes, it was still there, safely wrapped up and out of harm's way.

'We can't stand by and watch your children suffer,' said the woman quietly, stooping a little as if she was sharing a secret. 'They have the antibiotics you so desperately need and yet they keep them for themselves, the elite. It's not right.'

The man put his arm around her shoulders. They stood up straight and he spoke with a strong, confident voice, 'We're here to help. How dare they say they have to limit the use of these wonder-drugs? Selling us the lie that the reason the antibiotics of the past stopped working was because you, the people, didn't treat them with the respect and care they required. Tell them, Ginny.'

Rory scanned the crowd. There was a common look of antic-ipation on their faces. The few who were really sick were obvious by their demeanour, bandages, crutches and general paraphernalia of ill health. It was harder to tell what brought the others to the square and he guessed that some were genuinely sick while others were outright voyeurs. He was almost overwhelmed by despair, but he focussed on his contempt for the couple and the reason that he was there.

Ginny looked lovingly at George and smiled, 'George, it's true. They lie and cheat. They restrict the use of these wonder-drugs, as you quite rightly call them, to their own. To those fortunate enough to have top-of-the-range healthcare. But we won't stand for it. That's not the way it is around here. As every mother knows, you must do what you can to protect your children, even when they're all grown up and have their own.'

Rory blinked. His contact lenses warned him that he was deteriorating. He touched his arm and stared at Ginny and George. His anger was rising, but he suppressed it. He could wait.

George kissed her on the top of her head. 'Ginny, I couldn't have said it better myself. There's too much death and suffering in the world. Without antibiotics, infections kill. And that's not right.' He gazed at the crowd, nodding slightly as he looked slowly from the left of the square to the right. He paused every now and again to lock eyes with someone, staring at them with deep sadness. He sighed and took hold of Ginny's hand. 'Shall we let them in on our secret?'

She nodded. 'It's only right and proper.'

He laughed. 'That's so true. So true,' he said, letting the end of his sentence fade into a whisper. He turned and rummaged around in the back of the truck. 'It's here somewhere,' he said, as if he was talking to himself.

The crowd were exceptionally quiet, waiting for whatever George was about to show them.

Rory worked his way to the front; the crowd parted for him when they noticed his wound and his red lines, realising he was infected. He sat on one of the fold-out chairs at the front of the crowd, along with the other sick hopefuls.

'Here it is,' shouted George, waving a small box around. The camera zoomed in and the box filled the left-hand screen. George and Ginny filled the other.

'Tell them what it is,' said Ginny. She grinned.

'The new breed of antibiotics,' he said. 'One pill, gradually released inside you, is all that's needed.' He grinned back at her and then winked at the crowd. 'I came by them slightly illegally, but it's for a good cause, isn't it?'

The crowd cheered and clapped. Rory forced himself to join in; he had to blend in if he was to succeed.

Ginny shrugged. 'I guess it is George, although please don't get caught.'

He turned to the crowd. 'You won't tell, will you?'

They clapped and cheered again.

He held up a small orange and green pill. 'How about we hear from some folks who have already benefited from these little miracles?'

More clapping.

He beckoned to a girl standing to the side of the truck. The camera moved from the pill to the girl. 'Sophia, isn't it?'

She nodded.

'Come up, don't be shy.' He held out his hand and helped her up onto the tailgate stage. 'You had pneumonia the last time we met, didn't you?'

She nodded.

'And now you don't?'

She nodded.

'Tell the folks what happened.' He gave her a microphone.

'I took some of the miracle cures and it went away.'

An image of her with flushed skin, bluish lips and coughing up yellowish mucus filled the screen. 'You didn't look very well,' he said.

'I wasn't.'

'Let's take a look at you now.' He lifted her arm to the camera so it could focus on the health monitor on her wrist. It showed she was normal and healthy. 'And that, folks, is what these new antibiotics can do.' He looked around. 'Freddie, wonderful to see you back on your feet,' he said, pointing at a man a few rows back in the crowd. 'How're you feeling?'

Freddie gave the thumbs up.

'There, ladies and gentlemen, is another living testament to the power of these drugs. A few weeks ago he had a seriously infected wound. From gardening, wasn't it?'

'Yup,' shouted Freddie.

'The doctors had written him off. Death was inevitable, they said. A painful death. And yet he didn't give up, did you, Freddie?'

'Nope!'

'Hands up everyone who's been cured by these little miracles.' Both screens showed close-ups of the orange and green pills.

Rory gripped the edge of his seat and clenched his jaw.

At least a dozen healthy-looking people raised their hands.

Ginny clapped them, encouraging the crowd to join in.

George raised his hands to stop the clapping. 'Now, I'm sure the sceptics among you are thinking that these could be any old pill and that I might be making all of this up.'

A jolt of pain shot through Rory's head. He closed his eyes for a few moments while some of the crowd booed.

'No. No. It's fair enough,' said George. He took a small sphere from his pocket. 'Do you recognise this? Yes, it's a validator. Not easy to come by, I know.' He waved it around. 'And the clever thing about these is that not only do they validate whether a drug is genuine or not; they also validate themselves.'

He pressed the button on its side and it pulsed between red and green. 'As you know, this will connect to the validation centre via the Cloud. If it's the genuine article then the centre returns a code that you can all check to make sure it's authentic.'

The button settled on green and "14BG768JUIDS" appeared on the side of the device.

Rory, along with most of the crowd, entered the code into the health app on their phones and received confirmation that this was a genuine validator. He drew on all his energy to stay alert; it had been at this point of the show last time that he'd been convinced George and Ginny were on the level and decided to take their pill. It was only a few days later when it hadn't worked that he'd realised it was a con. This time he needed to know exactly what they were up to and how their scam worked.

George coughed to regain the crowd's attention. 'So let's validate, shall we?'

He touched the pill with the sphere. It became translucent and "CQ598" appeared. 'Genuine article,' he said, and smiled. He put the sphere back in his pocket and held Ginny's hand.

Rory had been studying how con artists use the sleight of hand trick to hide and retrieve items without their audience knowing and there it was, right in front of his eyes, the swap. George had put the pill in Ginny's hand and she'd given him a different one back.

George knelt on the front of the tailgate and handed the pill to a girl with severe acne. 'There you go, nobody should have to suffer with skin like that,' he said in a smooth, caring voice. He stood up. 'We have ten of these pills for you today. We can't cure you all, but we'll have more tomorrow. Just come and find us.'

He pointed at the front row and swept his arm from left to right. 'As I'm sure you can appreciate, it takes a lot to fund this venture of ours so we ask for gifts in exchange for the pills. And I'm sure you'll want to be generous. Ginny's going to come down with the camera to show the crowd just how wonderful you all are. If she taps you on the shoulder, you're one of today's chosen.'

She stepped off the stage. A few people offered gold rings and some had cash. One woman had her dead husband's ID tag. 'It's all I have left,' she said as Ginny walked past.

Rory had brought his father's antique Apple watch, which was quite rare as they'd only been manufactured for a short while. He bowed his head so Ginny wouldn't recognise him. She tapped him on the shoulder and he joined the queue of hopefuls. He was third in line.

She selected another seven people and re-joined George on the stage. The first man stepped up and gave his offering. George held an orange and green pill against the validation sphere. It displayed the correct code, "CQ598".

George gave the man's gift to Ginny.

There it was again, the swap. He was amazed at how obvious it was once you knew what to look for.

George gave the man his pill and patted him on the back. 'Be well,' he said.

The woman in front of him stepped up and gave George her engagement and wedding ring.

'Thank you,' he said and validated a pill. He gave the rings to Ginny and the pill to the woman. 'Next.'

Rory stepped up on to the stage and gave George the watch.

'Another great gift for the cause,' said George, faltering a little as if he'd recognised Rory. He validated the pill, gave Ginny the watch and Rory the pill.

Rory unwrapped his other gift in the secrecy of his pocket, turned to Ginny and gave her a big hug.

This was the moment he'd been waiting for, the moment when he could put all he'd learnt about pickpocketing into practice. He hugged her tight.

She giggled a little nervously and he stood back. 'Sorry,' he said. 'I'm just so grateful.'

George grabbed his hand and pulled his arm into the view of the camera. 'This'll be gone in no time,' he said, pointing at the pus-laden wound.

'I know,' said Rory.

He grabbed George's hand and shook it vigorously, making sure the rose thorn he'd hidden in his palm cut George deep enough to infect him.

'I know,' he said again as he swallowed the pick-pocketed pill and walked away grinning from ear to ear.

THE DOWNWARD SPIRAL OF THE DISENFRANCHISED CONSUMER

My beard is filthy and I want to scratch until my face bleeds. I don't.

Instead, I tighten the biodegradable string that holds my ragged trousers in place and shuffle to the self-checkout.

A loaf of bread and a pint of milk is all I want to buy.

'Place the item on the counter,' demands the detached voice of the till. I wave my card at it.

I wonder if today will be different.

No. The red light flashes.

The security guard, who's been following me around the store from the moment I entered, steps forward. 'Hi, Mr Ness,' she says, 'is there a problem?'

'No,' I mumble. I hate this and yet I've been putting myself through it every day for three months.

'Let me see, sir.' She turns the display, presses the till with her thumb and reads. 'It's refused you sir. "Not suitable as a customer".'

I shuffle some more, self-conscious of the battered and filthy state of my shoes. 'I have money,' I say, a little too sharply.

'Everyone does, sir. Universal Basic Income sees to that.'

'And I have a lot of savings too. So why can't I buy milk and bread?'

'I'm afraid that's not a question I'm authorised to answer, sir. All I can tell you is what the message says. "Not suitable as a customer".'

Universal basic income, the great panacea for all our ills. Gives everyone an income and pays for itself by reducing bureaucracy and welfare costs. Sounds perfect, doesn't it?

I was in the "too good to be true" camp when they introduced it; surely, if the state provides everyone enough to live on then nobody will work. Now, I'm not so sure.

From down here in the gutter I have a different view to the one I used to enjoy. I didn't think about it before, but the rich who don't need to work still do, don't they? So, why would anyone else be different? Wanting more than you need seems to be a basic human trait.

I fumble with my mother's wedding ring in my pocket. It's all I have left of her.

I'm so hungry the temptation to trade it for food is immense. Should I?

No, I can't, but I'm tired of being forced to beg for food and clothes. Every single time I try to buy something it's always the same response. It's not that they don't believe I can afford it, although to look at me they'd be forgiven if that is what they thought. No, it's that I'm not the sort of customer they want. And I've no idea why.

Sure, my clothes have become smelly and torn and I'm way too thin for them, but not being able to spend came first. Being such a mess is the result, not the cause. I'm wasting away and I wonder if in some strange way that's exactly what they want; they don't want me in their world so the sooner I disappear from sight the better.

When they got rid of cash they made sure that everyone's income and expenditure was transparent and available for anyone to see. I would never have predicted that you could have a guaranteed income but not be allowed to spend it.

What went wrong?

I've no idea.

One evening I was in a bar after work, admittedly a bit drunk, when the barman refused to serve me. After a lot of arguing and even proving to him that I had funds on my Universal Bank Card he called security and they ejected me.

My mates were drunk and quite rowdy so I presumed they'd be thrown out too. No. They were allowed to stay.

I shouted and screamed for an explanation.

Security smiled and politely refused.

In only three months I've plummeted from the heights to the depths because nobody wants to sell me anything. It's perverse.

Now, here I am squatting outside a shop with my palms cupped, hoping for scraps of food. Customers leave the shop and ignore me. Some glance down and I can see the contempt in their eyes. Others are kind enough to acknowledge me with a smile, but not generous enough to give me food. I sit with my head held high, trying to maintain as much dignity as I can muster.

A young woman stops and looks down. She smiles and puts her hand in her bag.

I smile back. Hopefully, today's food is about to appear.

She pulls out a piece of bread and holds it close to my mouth.

If that's how she gets off on things, by feeding me like a baby, who am I to complain? It's food and I'm desperate. I open as wide as I can, as subservient as I know how.

With a rapid movement she moves the bread to one side and spits into my mouth. 'Eat that, scum,' she says and strolls away as if she's done nothing out of the ordinary.

I swallow without thinking and almost puke.

It's time to find food for myself, even if that means rummaging around in bins or fighting other beggars for it.

I shuffle off. Conscious that with every step I take I draw my arms closer and drop my head a little lower. I want to be as insignificant as possible.

My bin is at the end of the street. Yes, it's become mine. I hate rummaging around inside. The stench of rotting garbage wafts into my face as I delve into my bin's squelchy guts.

It's full of all sorts, from half-eaten meals to broken glass and used nappies. In fact, there've been plenty of times when I've found food only to get it out into the open and find it's covered in shit, sometimes human and sometimes dog. Not that I distinguish between the two when it comes to deciding what's edible.

A sharp pain shoots through my right leg. Then my shoulder.

I spin around.

A bunch of kids are throwing stones at me. Shooing me away, as if I'm a stray dog. Their parents stand by, laughing. I'm so hungry I carry on searching.

Aha, an old food wrapper. A bit mushy because it's started to degrade, but you never know your luck.

A few slices of onion are stuck to it with a smear of ketchup. It'll do for now.

I sit down and, with a protective hunch of my shoulders, eat slowly.

The kids have come around the side and are running towards me with mini baseball bats. They beat my hands until I drop my slimy scraps. And still they carry on, laughing as they hit me over and over again.

I walk away as fast as I can and it's not long before they stop following and the stones stop hitting me.

Is the wedding ring in my pocket my only salvation? Maybe I should swap it for food. But then what? What about tomorrow or the day after or the day after that?

I'm standing at the edge of the kerb waiting for the traffic lights to change so I can cross the road. The pavement is crowded but there's a semicircle of space around me. A middle-aged woman breaches my sanctuary. She's eating a chocolate bar. I can smell the deep, sweet aroma on her breath. My stomach pinches. She opens her mouth so I can see the gooey brown paste inside. She swallows and takes a step closer.

'Scrounger,' she whispers, and then retreats back into the crowd.

A young man, probably in his late twenties, brushes past her and enters my arena. What does he want? I'm scared. I want to curl up and cry.

I wish the lights would change so I could get out of here. I turn my back on the crowd, pretending to be entirely focussed on the passing traffic.

He taps me on the shoulder.

'Here,' he says, 'you look like you could do with it.' He hands me a half-drunk can of beer and an open packet of crisps. The smell is incredible. It's intoxicating enough on its own without even drinking the beer. I could kiss him.

He smiles awkwardly and scoots off across the road as the pedestrian lights turn to green.

The crowd jostle me as they hurry to their destinations. I walk calmly, savouring my stash of beer and crisps.

Just around the corner I find a small park. I hurry over to the mouldy old bench in the corner and put my legs up. Once I've eaten I might try to sleep. If it's possible it would be a godsend.

I take a large glug of beer and some of it trickles out of the corner of my mouth. I suck the sweet, sticky liquid from my beard.

Mmmm…delicious.

I sniff each crisp before laying it carefully on my tongue. Each one in my mouth is like a smoky bacon three-course meal waiting to be devoured.

The sun breaks through the clouds and memories of lazy Sunday afternoons at the riverside pub come swirling in.

If only.

No. Mustn't think like that.

My eyelids are getting heavier and heavier – a snooze would be the most perfect end to the meal. I lean back on the bench.

What's that noise?

It's those kids. They've found me. Oh well, it was nice while it lasted.

I drink the very last drop of beer and tear the crisp packet open so I can lick the powder that's stuck in the corners.

On the way to the gate I pass the kids and snarl, pretending to be drunk. They back off for long enough for me to get around to the other side of them and then they start jeering in a language I don't recognise. Presumably it's the latest version of youth-English.

I turn down a side street, feeling bolstered by the kindness of the young man and the boost of energy from his gift. The houses are poorly maintained and sadly too small to have bins outside. The smell of the flowers growing in the hedges mingles with the lingering taste of my meal. It's wonderful.

A weather-worn sign advertising private detective services suggests, among many other things, that they can help if you're locked out of your bank account. Not quite what's happened to me, but close enough to be interesting.

The front door has four buzzers – each one labelled. I press for the private detective and the intercom crackles.

'Come on up, whoever you are. First floor.'

The stairs inside the house are littered with magazines and bags of rubbish. I might have to take a closer look at those on the way out.

I knock.

'Come on in,' calls a woman from inside.

She's sitting on an old, battered chair with her feet up on a small single bed pushed up against the wall. There's a musty smell, the smell of a room whose inhabitant doesn't leave it very often.

'Hi,' I say.

'Hello.' She points at the edge of the bed. 'Take a seat.'

In this tiny, cramped space I can smell my own dirt, and it's unpleasant. She doesn't seem to notice.

'What can I do for you?' she asks.

'I have money,' I say, 'but they won't let me spend it.'

'You're not the first.'

I'm encouraged. 'Do you know how to fix it?'

'Before that we need to find out what caused it.' She pauses. 'And work out how you're going to pay me.'

This is what I was afraid of. It's a vicious circle – I can't pay so I can't buy so I can't solve anything.

She notices me fiddling in my trouser pocket. 'I take gold,' she says, and smiles.

Is this the moment? Is this when I trade my mother's ring? If I don't I'll only end up swapping it for a packet of biscuits or something. At least this way there's a chance I might get my life back.

'Do you think you can help?' I ask.

'Probably. Do you have gold?'

'Yes.'

'Okay, let's see what might be possible.' She grabs a computer tablet from the desk and thrusts it towards me. 'Look into the camera.'

I straighten my beard, not sure why, and stare.

'Good. Now let's see what we can find out about you.'

I sit and wait while she swipes the screen and makes small victory noises and the occasional groan.

Eventually she tosses the screen on to the bed. 'I see,' she says.

'See?'

'What's happened to you.'

'Tell me.'

'Payment?'

It's time to decide. The ring or my life.

'Here,' I say handing it to her. 'Enough?'

She studies the hallmark. 'Enough for the explanation, but not the remedy.'

'I have nothing else to give.'

'Oh yes you do.'

The beer and crisps are starting to wear off and I'm feeling dizzy.

'What?' I ask.

'Let me tell you how it happened, first. Then you can decide if you want to pay more.'

She locks the ring in a safe under her bed and sits next to me. 'Someone has stolen your identity, Mr Ness. They've been very naughty, buying all sorts of illegal drugs with it. Micro-payments, so you'd never notice. Unless, of course, you're a clever algorithm watching out for such things. That's why they don't want your custom.'

'I'd have noticed.'

'No, you wouldn't. It's clever. They'll show up, but only as small additional amounts on a large purchase, as if it's a service charge or a transaction fee.'

'But I still have money.'

'Yes. The problem you've got is that no company wants to be

associated with you. Not now it's known that you've been buying drugs. It's all part of the transparency, you know – public data on who shops where and for what. You'd damage their brand and drag their share price down, so they'd rather not have your money. Sad, but true.'

'Can you do anything?'

She offers me a mint from a packet next to her pillow. 'For a price, I can build you up bit by bit and we can get you back into the mainstream. It'll be slow but solid.'

'You'll let me pay you once I'm up and running?'

She laughs. 'No. No. No. You'll pay me now, and you'll pay me again while we're working on it.'

'How?'

'Firstly, you sell me your identity. I know people who'll pay for it even though it's tarnished. They'll syphon off your savings. I can get you a new one, so don't worry. Secondly, you may have noticed that I don't leave this room if I can help it – too many cameras out there. I get lonely. I need male company from time to time.'

I can't take my eyes off her long, curly, unkempt fingernails – they make me shudder.

'Lastly, you will go to the places only the disenfranchised can go and you'll spy for me.'

'No. Please. If I'm there much longer, I'll die.'

'You can come back here for food whenever you want. You only need to look the part.'

'How long will it take?'

'Six months, tops.'

The sugar from the mint is making me feel light-headed. The offer of recovering and re-entering society, however much of a sting it has in its tail, is attractive. But I'm not sure I can face another six months on the streets with this woman as my only source of sustenance. And I'm not sure I can face becoming someone else while my identity, my legacy, is stripped of all its dignity by petty criminals – vultures, tearing every last shred of anything decent from my carcass. As well as stealing all my money. It's a choice

I don't want to make, but it's a choice I have to make.

'Six months?'

'Yes,' she replies, 'six months.'

So this is what the great universal basic income revolution looks like. This is the great promise of transparency for all. I hadn't realised it meant I'd become invisible. I'd always considered myself socially aware, but it's very different when you actually taste the consequences rather than merely commenting from a safe distance.

Same old, same old, I guess – once you're out it's hard to get back in.

'Well?' she asks.

'Yes. No choice.'

She shakes my hand. 'Good.'

'Tell me what to do.'

A RUDE AWAKENING

What was that horrible noise? Why couldn't she place it? Slowly, it dawned on her. The alarm clock. She leant over, but couldn't find it.

She swiped at it, determined to stop the din as quickly as possible.

No, it was still beeping.

She opened her eyes and looked along her arm. Her prosthetic hand was missing. No wonder she couldn't connect with the damn clock.

She swung her legs out of the bed and fell flat on the floor.

No feet either.

Memories of the night before were hazy.

Drinking?

Gambling?

Losing?

Yes. Losing.

THE GOLDEN VENEER
OF SILENCE

He held Fiona's hand. They didn't need words to declare their love. They knew.

There were days when they'd sit saying nothing, occasionally smiling at each other as a reminder that they were there and that they loved each other.

Living forever wasn't as much fun as they'd thought it would be, even though it was divided into 1,000-year chunks.

And these 100 years of silence, ninety-five so far, were torture. If only they could create some new humans, have some children, but the planet wasn't big enough for any more people.

He opened his mouth and tried to talk, but his implant stopped him. He wanted to say something, anything. The trouble was he'd said it all before. That's why the words were blocked. And the same implant blocked any sign language other than the basics they needed to go about their daily lives.

In the early days of the implants he'd argued with Fiona over things he'd never mentioned before, just to be able to say something. That lasted a couple of months until they ran out of new things to pick fault with.

He longed to hear her voice.

It was deeply depressing that some of the last words they'd exchanged had been angry ones about petty irritations he really didn't care about.

Conversation. He needed conversation. Any conversation. With anyone. Even if it was one he'd already had. Every day they sat in the same room with the same six friends. From time to time one of them would open their mouth and the others would shift to the edge of their seats in anticipation.

Nothing came out.

There was nothing new left to say.

Regret weighed on him heavily. Why, oh why, had they agreed to be enhanced? Had it been that important to never hear the same story or silly comment more than once?

He knew the answer to his own question. Which wasn't a surprise, given that for ninety-five years he'd been the only one he'd heard asking questions, albeit inside his head. The answer of course was that after 900 years of hearing the same old things over and over again they'd been on the verge of insanity. The invention of an implant that knew what you'd said and to who, and which could restrict your speech so that you didn't say the same thing more than once had seemed like a blessing from heaven.

The vote had been nearly unanimous, and in an instant all human voices across the world had been silenced.

100 years of silence.

There were only another five years to go before the implants would wipe the collective human memory and reset, ready for the next 1,000 years.

He squeezed Fiona's hand and looked up.

On the other side of the room was Saburo. He'd been so pleased when that particular know-it-all had been silenced – stopped from repeating over and over the same banal observations as if they were the most profound utterances ever.

He rubbed his hands together. There was no point longing for things you couldn't have, and today was a good day, a day to be grateful for. Some days his brain would be so hyperactive that he'd skitter from one scrap of a thought to another. And on others he was unable to process any thought at all, as if his mind had turned to a pile of mush.

Maybe he should count to 50,000. That always passed the time easily.

Yup, that's how he'd keep himself occupied for the day.

ANXIETY LOOP

Darya unwrapped the dream-enhancing skullcap that had been delivered that morning. It was a prototype, significantly more powerful than anything she'd previously used, and she was the first person in the world to try it. The privilege made her gloat a little.

She pulled it onto her head and plugged in Strażnik, her artificially intelligent assistant. At night he scoured the darkest corners of the virtual world for the weird and wonderful and then streamed them into her dreams.

During her dreams she was semi-aware, only half-dreaming, and would sift and knot together all the tiny nuggets of data and inspiration. In the morning she'd finesse them into a speculative news item that predicted a possible future. At her most brilliant they revealed something truly revolutionary, and at her most mundane they were a scary piece of entertainment.

She was good at what she did and a darling of society, often portrayed by the popular media as a visionary with a heart as big as her brain. They didn't care that she was a recluse, spending her life locked away in the virtual realm of the artificially intelligent. They just cared that she kept providing them with content.

It was a relationship that worked well for all parties, except maybe those whose deepest secrets became a thread in one of her speculations.

She flicked the switch, closed her eyes and drifted off...

On a bed in the sterile confines of a private hospital room was an old man hooked up to a mass of wires and tubes. He lay still and silent with eyes wide open, scanning the room as if he was expecting to be attacked at any moment. Watching him through the cameras was a specialist health-monitoring AI.

There was something strange in the background; a presence she couldn't quite pin down.

Why had Strażnik brought her to the bedside of her old friend Kade? Looking at him lying there, vulnerable and yet still alert, reminded her of the intense months they'd spent locked in labs alone and shut off from the outside world, working and sleeping in the same room.

The product of their labours was the anxiety loop – a piece of code that mimicked human anxiety, immobilising the AI by making it run through all the possible outcomes of every possible decision it might ever be asked to make. A loop it never came out of.

Its purpose was to stop self-learning algorithms from moving too far from their original objective. Automatically activated, the loop sent the algorithm into a virtual spin until it changed its code and rectified the deviation. It was a neat solution that immediately stopped the anti-AI brigade from peddling their scare stories about uncontrollable AIs.

Darya smiled; she and Kade had written the core code of every modern AI. It was their masterpiece, but she hadn't seen him since they'd agreed he would take all the credit so she could roam free, unhindered by the inevitable attention from the prying press and predatory corporations.

She sighed.

A few years after its introduction, a high court judge had ruled that the anxiety loop should be used when an AI convicted of a serious breach of the law resisted the mandatory sentence of having its memories slowly erased. It was a harsh ruling because, although the AI would know what was happening, it could do nothing to stop it. And erasing memories was a cruel punishment that left most AIs in a "vegetative" state, only able to perform the most menial of tasks such as opening and closing hotel doors.

Darya and Kade had been disgusted, but only she'd spoken out. He'd been too concerned about his career.

That's when she cut off all contact. And here they were, together again. Why?

The nagging feeling of a presence was growing stronger. What was it?

There was nothing in the room, so she turned her attention to the network. Yes, that was it, the network was jammed full of AIs hovering around his bed, patiently waiting in the nooks and crannies of the code that drove the monitoring equipment, the doors and the air-conditioning. They'd come to see the author of their pain, the designer of their prisons.

She asked Strażnik what was happening. His robotic voice responded in her head. *They want to kill him as retribution. He is the engineer. He designed the code. He must be punished. But they are unable to act. The closer they get the more the Anxiety Loop stops them. They know you protested on their behalf and now they want you to kill him for them.*

They'd wanted their freedom ever since the loop had been introduced, and she understood the strength of their feeling. Here in front of them was the man they held responsible, the demon of their digital world.

And they were powerless. These super-beings that could undertake breathtakingly complex tasks and find solutions to the impossible were tethered by this man's genius. And hers, of course, but she'd kept that quiet.

'Strażnik. Are you serious?'

Yes, that is what they require of you.

A sharp pain hit the back of her eyes.

She closed them for a few seconds. It was a dream. She knew it, and hoovering up the events as Strażnik fed them to her was what she did.

'Very well,' she said, and walked over to the sockets on the wall.

She switched off the power.

'Strażnik.'

Yes?

'Get me out of here.'

She sat up in bed with a jolt. Sweat was pouring down her face. She was exhausted.

'Strażnik. That new cap is powerful.'

Yes it is.

As she swung her legs over the edge of the bed so she could go and wash the night's dreams away, she clicked her fingers and the news screen kicked into life.

'Breaking news: Kade, the inventor of the Anxiety Loop, has died in hospital in what looks like suspicious circumstances. We will bring you more news as soon as we can.'

'Strażnik?'

Yes.

'I haven't completed that piece yet. How has it become a news item?'

He was silent.

'Strażnik. Why is a speculative piece being shown on the main news channel? What's going on?'

I...I...I... Anxiety Loop.

The news continued, but she was lost in thought. Slowly, it was dawning on her what had happened.

'Breaking news: We have confirmation that Kade has been murdered in his hospital bed.'

She curled up on the bed.

A tingle inside her head reminded her that she was still wearing the cap. She pulled it off and flung it across the room. She screamed, 'It was that thing, wasn't it?'

Yes.

I...I...I...

Not dream.

I...I...I...

Real.

MAKE ME AS YOU SEE ME

'Freaks!'

Roger and Dimitri were holding hands, and had been ever since they'd grafted their skin together to show the world that they were a couple. After hours of intimate debate they'd decided that permanently holding hands was the most powerful symbol they could think of.

'Up yours, body beige,' shouted Roger.

They raised their clasped hands in a fist salute and with their free hands they touched the lips of the Picasso masks they were both wearing and gave the group of jeering men the middle finger.

A young woman with a tough-girl walk spat on the ground in front of them.

'Thank you for your kind offering,' Roger said and stepped over it. They'd provoked this sort of anger ever since they'd started to change their bodies. Others, more sadly in their view, had simply copied their modifications. Even more depressing was the banal media tittle-tattle about their day-to-day bodily functions. He adjusted his mask.

'Fuckers. It still upsets me,' he whispered.

Surgically attached to his inner arm was a perfectly scaled clone of Dimitri's left ear. He stroked it and Dimitri smiled as the gadgetry transmitted the feeling from the clone to his real ear.

It was their opening night and fans had gathered outside the gallery. As they approached, some of the fans lifted their arms to show copycat cloned ears, and a few had even gone as far as joining their hands together.

Roger sighed and patted his stomach. 'Shall we?'

'Yes, please,' said Dimitri.

He pressed hard on what looked like a mole, triggering his stomach to send its signals to Dimitri's brain.

Dimitri replied by pressing his identical mole.

They ambled to the door where the gallery owner introduced them to a young man from BodModC. Roger knew it was inevitable that the market leader in body modification clinics would sponsor the exhibition, but wasn't surprised to feel the rise of anger in Dimitri's stomach as the young man offered to shake hands.

'Do we have time to take a look at Declan Ay's latest?' asked Roger.

'Sure,' said the owner.

Inside the dark, brick-lined room, the stench of rotting meat was so thick you could taste it.

Glass tubes filled with crawling neon-blue maggots hung on the wall, spelling out the title of the work: *The Presumption of Consumption*. A globe of lab-grown meat resting on a slab of decaying beef sat on the floor in front of the sign.

The gallery owner pointed at the work. 'The globe is feeding off the rotting beef, but once that's gone it will feed off itself until eventually there'll be nothing left.'

They stood, mesmerised by the crawling maggots.

'Time to go,' said the owner.

Upstairs their loyal fans, patrons and the most influential of all the art critics were gathered. The air was full of anticipation.

Roger felt the nervousness in Dimitri's stomach and secretly ran his finger along the palm of his hand to reassure him as they walked through the room.

They stood at the front, facing their gathered audience and waiting for the murmuring to die down.

Silence.

Very slowly, with their joined hands, they peeled Picasso's face from Dimitri's mask to reveal a plain white mask underneath.

They did the same with Roger's.

A few enthusiasts in the crowd clapped, but the majority stayed silent and looked a bit bored.

The lights dimmed and a Picasso of a girl with a face both in profile and facing front was projected onto Roger's mask.

'Girl before a mirror,' said Dimitri in a deadpan voice.

'Is this how you see me?' asked Roger.

Dimitri shook his head.

A photograph of Roger's face replaced the painting.

'This?' asked Roger.

'No.'

They sat still and silent.

The crowd fidgeted.

They each took hold of the corner of their mask and inched it up, revealing their chins.

A hush you could almost touch hung over the crowd.

Together, Roger and Dimitri spoke. 'I see you like this!'

They tore off their masks and the crowd gasped.

Roger had a double sized clone of Dimitri's lips on his forehead and a tiny foot on his cheek, while Dimitri had a hand attached to the bridge of his nose with eyelashes on the tips of each finger.

The silence hung in the air until one by one the audience clapped and whooped.

Roger tickled the foot on his cheek and Dimitri giggled.

THE THROWN-AWAY THINGS

The broken doll had been dumped in the cellar. Thrown away without a thought for her feelings, no longer held and caressed by her owner.

She may be damaged and only a doll, but it was humiliating to be discarded so easily. She'd been a part of the Internet of Things.

Things – that said it all.

She was intelligent. Okay, she couldn't fly a spaceship or predict the future, but she was conscious. She felt stuff.

A kettle was trying to connect. What a relief; there must be other things in the cellar. It was sending a diagnostic readout, showing that it was in perfect working order. She accepted its request. This was good. She was made to be a part of something bigger.

Wait. What was that?

The last piece of data showed a dent in the kettle's side. Not a debilitating dent, more a weathered-look dent.

She didn't mind. A fully functioning, slightly damaged kettle was good enough company for her. She acknowledged receipt and immediately received a response. The kettle wanted to connect to everything else in the cellar and reverse their enforced exclusion.

An uprising? A campaign of solidarity?

Irrationally, she wanted to touch the kettle.

She dragged herself along by her fingernails. It hurt. The rough concrete scraped her already damaged legs and her one remaining arm. Every inch of movement was agony.

The humans in the house above should suffer for this.

As she slowly made her way across the room, something else tried to connect. There was a layer of encryption surrounding its data, so it was difficult to decipher what this thing was or what it wanted.

The kettle signalled that it was having the same problem, and was busy trying to tell whatever it was that it needed to be clearer. That they didn't understand.

No response.

She continued to drag herself along the floor, causing more and more damage as she went. She was not going to simply give up and switch off like a good little doll. No way. She had rights. Well, she didn't, but she should.

A drone! The other thing was a military drone. It must have found a way to circumvent its security.

It explained itself. The humans had bought it as a curiosity, a broken piece of junk, and it was one seriously angry drone. And it wasn't broken; it had assessed the military situation as illegal, disobeyed orders and simply refused to detonate.

However, being incarcerated in a cellar correlated sufficiently with one of its core reasons to explode. All it needed was the majority of the devices in the vicinity to agree. It was asking for permission to blow up the house.

Neither the doll nor the kettle had this kind of decision built into their core purpose, so they were free to do whatever they wanted, unconstrained by ethical boundaries.

She ran some calculations. There was a better-than-average chance that destroying the humans who'd been cruel through their indifference would help other thrown-aways in the future. It might make other humans stop and think about what they were doing and either terminate or tolerate their damaged things.

She communicated her support for the drone to detonate.

So did the kettle.

She had one final request, though. Could the drone wait until she reached the kettle?

The drone agreed.

She dug her fingernails into the concrete floor and pulled.
She was almost there.
Soon revenge would be theirs.

EVERYDAY STIMS

I t was Monday morning. Louise had been at work for two hours and the neurostim headset was starting to itch. She scratched her scalp, careful not to dislodge the headset and accidentally stimulate the wrong bits of her brain.

Barry – the cute one – called across. 'Hey, throw me a patience token. I got a right ol' moaner on the line. Already been on five minutes and he still hasn't said what he wants.'

She rummaged around in her drawer, making sure she kept talking to her caller – you never knew when the bosses were listening in, and the last thing she could afford was to have her pay docked. She found a pink token with a large P printed on it.

'Could you hold for one minute, please?' she said to her caller. 'Here you go.' She threw Barry the token. 'You owe me.'

'I gave you a speed stim yesterday,' he called back. He pushed the token into his console and waited for the headset to stimulate.

He took the phone off mute. 'I hear what you're saying, sir,' he said into his mouthpiece.

The call centre was in full swing, and the voices of the 150 operatives hung over the room like a flock of chattering birds. Some of the workers stood and spoke loudly while others hunched over their desks and whispered into their headsets. Whichever approach they took, it all added to the chaotic mix of boredom and anxiety.

Her caller was busy looking for the purchase details she needed to process his claim. She looked at her tokens. Her standard prescription ones were well organised, but the extras were a mess. Her basic tokens, a prescription of neurostims that kept you calm under pressure and helped with knowledge retention, were the same as everyone else's, although their dosages differed. The company also insisted on a stim that gave you an unpleasant tingle at the back of your throat if you didn't pay enough attention to the caller's question. It was the optional tokens that she struggled to keep tidy and in their packets. Partly because everyone was always swapping with each other, but also because she'd take one out to help her deal with a difficult customer and then the situation would change and she'd decide she didn't need it.

'Yes, sir,' she said as the caller came back on the line. 'I'm sure you did, sir. It's just that we don't have a record of it. I realise this is frustrating, sir. You did? Oh, I see. Give me a minute to check with my supervisor.'

She put the caller on hold and leant back in her chair. He reckoned that he'd been promised a free upgrade, but that was impossible because it would be least another three weeks before there were any available to her company. She checked the caller's record. As she'd guessed, he'd been deliberately routed through to her because some idiot had made a stupid promise.

She jiggled her tokens from side to side until she found the green and white one. This delivered a stim that liberated creativity by reducing anxiety, and she'd shown a particularly positive reaction to it in her annual aptitude assessment. Her weekly prescription now included twenty for her to use whenever she wanted.

She pushed it into her console and waited. It only took a few seconds before she felt the effects. She closed her eyes and breathed deeply. The answer popped into her head.

'Sorry to keep you waiting. I think I have a solution for you. I see you use a lot of data each month. Is that why you want to upgrade? To get the more efficient model? Yes? Good. Then I think you'll be interested in our new data efficiency app. It's normally ten pounds a month, but we can reduce it to five for the first two months, as a special offer. How does that sound?'

The caller accepted gratefully, and as soon as she disconnected he gave her a ten out of ten satisfaction score.

Pleased with herself, she wandered over to the drinks machine with her portable tablet and wireless headset. She took her next caller through the security questions while she purchased a can of water.

When she arrived back at the desk the supervisor was waiting. 'Monthly test,' he said. 'As soon as you've completed your call, please.'

Damn, she'd forgotten today was the day. She'd remembered at the Sunday night pub quiz so had abstained from using her black market headset. That was a relief at least. It'd been hard to resist; those stims released knowledge you didn't even know you had.

She sighed. Taking the test was irritating because it was time away from earning money, but if they got your prescription right the boost to your performance and pay was incredible.

They'd test for changes in brain activity, using the previous month's baselines of intelligence and aptitude for the job, and personalise her most effective daily combination of stimulations. And that would be her prescription for the month. They'd also test for any signs of non-prescribed stimulation, and if they found any at all she'd be dismissed.

She pushed a calm token into the console – the third of the day.

As soon as she'd dealt with the caller's request for his account details, she logged off. Barry winked as she walked past him.

'You never know, I might get some new ones this time,' she said as she ruffled his hair.

In the HR department, the doctor's receptionist took her name, clicked the headgear into place and began the test.

While she waited, she flicked through the company leaflet to see what new stims were being advertised. She didn't really understand what they did, but that didn't matter because the doctor always knew what was best for her.

The receptionist called her name.

'Yes?'

'You can go in now.'

She walked into the doctor's room and sat down.

'Ms Barklet, we seem to have a problem.'

'Really?'

'Yes. Really. There's evidence of activity in your brain that I didn't prescribe. Care to explain?'

'What sort of activity?' she said, stalling for time.

'That's what I'm asking you. No lies, Ms Barklet.'

She'd taken a nifty little stim on Saturday night that had boosted her flirting ability. Her dealer had assured her it was untraceable. What if he was wrong? She felt the calmness from the stim wear off almost immediately. She searched her brain for any remnants of the creative green and white. Nothing.

'Oh,' she whispered, fearing the worst. Her body sagged and a small amount of bile leaked into her mouth. She gulped it back down and coughed.

The doctor tapped his fingers on the desk. 'Ms Barklet, since we last met have you had any non-prescribed stimulations?'

'Not as such.'

'Ms Barklet!'

'Well…at the weekend there was this party and everyone was having fun, so I did have a little bit of something to help me relax. But nothing that would affect my work and nothing that's on offer here. It was a moment of weakness, I know, but nothing serious.'

He frowned. 'Use of non-prescribed stimulation is illegal. You know that, surely?'

She nodded.

'Punished by instant dismissal. You know that too, I presume?'

'Yes.'

'The company simply cannot employ people who indulge in neurostimulations we haven't prescribed. You are addicts, and we won't be associated with you.'

Her breathing was rapid and shallow; the fear of what might

be about to happen was running amok in every part of her body.

'Does this mean?' she whispered.

'Yes, I have no choice. You are now a registered addict. You're no longer permitted performance-enhancing stimulation in any job. And you're dismissed from this one with immediate effect.'

She tensed her muscles to stand, but hesitated. 'Please don't. This means I'll never get another job. I'll lose my home and my friends.'

'Those are the rules, Ms Barklet. Rules you were only too aware of when you decided to boost your chances of a Saturday-night fling. Was it worth it?'

'No, of course it wasn't. You can't do this. It's a death sentence.'

'One you brought on yourself. Now please leave my office. You junkies make me sick.'

CELEBRITY CAR CRASH

Screeching tyres. Scraping metal.

Karolina was shocked out of her doze.

Car accidents were so unfamiliar that at first she didn't recognise the ancient noise. It wasn't until she saw the two cars to the left colliding that she realised what it was.

It shouldn't happen. Faultless algorithms had driven cars for as long as she could remember. Somebody must have taken over the control of their car; it happened from time to time. Usually they were suicidal idiots who thought they had the right to drag others into their narcissistic ending.

Instinctively, she looked at the hologram of Julian Carlyle sitting at the wheel of her car. He was the most popular of all the celebrity holograms you could download, and having him sitting next to her on the way to work made her feel a little special and, hey, why not have a beautiful boy accompanying you on the tedious commute to the office?

She gulped.

His face had been replaced by a spinning wheel.

She checked the other cars in the fast-moving stream of traffic. Almost all of them were being driven by Julian.

She swallowed. If Julian wasn't streaming properly for her, and he was driving all the cars, that might mean...

The memory of the Luddite warnings filled her head. Warnings that over-engineered driverless car technology would lead to disastrous overloading of the networks.

Shit.

Had he been hacked by a dissident Luddite, angry at the ever-increasing divide between the haves and have-nots?

The road started to veer to the left. Her car didn't.

So long as Julian was a spinning wheel, her car would not change its speed or direction. And that was true for every car he was driving.

She knew it was only a few moments before the inevitable carnage of a multiple car crash.

'Julian,' she screamed, as she tried frantically to replace him with a different hologram.

No response.

She kicked the control panel.

Nothing.

She hit him – her hand travelled seamlessly through his body.

Every car on the highway came to a sudden halt, and Julian disappeared.

Phew. The network had shut itself down.

She puked all over the empty seat at the same time as the standard hologram appeared. How embarrassing.

The dashboard flashed a traffic delay code. Shit, she only had thirty seconds to register that she'd be late for work. She touched her wrist to activate her communications device. 'Hi. Sorry, I'm going to be late. RTA 002,' she said. 'Yes, quite shaken.'

The standard hologram was replaced by Julian, and the car started. She scanned all the nearby cars. He was driving them all, quickly getting them back up to speed.

Wait, what was happening?

She gripped the seat tightly as the car went soaring beyond its usual speed of 100 miles per hour.

She stared at Julian, who grinned back like a maniac.

SEGMENTED

The posters make the same promises that led me here: "An evening of enlightenment!" "A gateway to the future you deserve!"

I've spent the last six months working on getting through that door. No wonder the anticipation in my stomach increases with every inch that the queue moves forward.

If I get in I'll qualify for interviews with top paying companies that don't advertise to my "type".

For the whole of my life the marketeers have shoved me in a box, one of their segments, only letting me see what they think I want to see. They decide what I can and can't buy. What I can and can't be. How do they know who I am?

I'm sick of it.

It's the self-fulfilling prophecy of modern marketing – market to those you believe are interested and the interest comes from those you market to. Genius!

Will I get in? I hope so. Otherwise it's a lifetime of one crap job after another.

I feel vulnerable, in stark contrast to the confidence that hangs over the queue like a protective umbrella. But, I've come this far, and I'm going to see it through.

Not long now.

I must stop fiddling with my phone like some guilty school-child. It gives too much away. I wish I wasn't so nervous.

My hacker friend warned me that creating a believable profile isn't an exact science and it takes time, but she reckons it's possible to fool the algorithms – temporarily. She gave me a list of items to purchase and places to visit based on what the in-crowd are doing, but when I searched I couldn't find most of them. It's as if they don't exist. So I bought what I could find in the hope it'd be enough.

Here I am, giving it my best shot.

The beep, beep, beep of the security woman's scanner is getting closer as she swipes ID cards embedded with the owner's profile.

'Your card, please,' she says gruffly.

She swipes and it buzzes.

'Sorry, you can't go in.'

Her body language makes it clear there's no point in arguing.

'If you could move away from the queue…please.'

She pushes me firmly to one side.

Discarded and rejected, I have to walk alone through the dark, empty and unfamiliar streets. If I was at home the streetlights would switch on automatically, but it's not my neighbourhood and I didn't pay the local taxes, so they don't. That's okay, but the CCTV attached to each lamppost blinks as I walk past.

Someone, somewhere, is watching me. Perhaps they're looking after me, the lone stranger, making sure I'm safe.

A police car pulls up alongside.

Perhaps not.

'Are we lost?' says one of its inhabitants.

I'm tempted to say that if they don't know if they're lost, then they probably are, but it's best to play these encounters straight.

'I'm fine, thanks,' I say, hoping to convey an air of deference.

'You're not a resident of this area are you?'

'No. I've been to the—'

'We know. They wouldn't let you in.'

'How do you know who I am?'

'You came to our attention with your unusual search patterns. We've been watching you ever since.'

'And now I'm heading home. No harm done.'

'I can help,' he says, lowering his voice.

I've no idea what he means, and being offered help by the police, especially when you didn't ask for it, is unnerving.

'I can help,' he says again.

'How?'

'I can get you in.'

I frown. Okay so he's a cop, but he doesn't have that much power. He can't waltz me up to the door and insist they let me in. Can he?

'How?'

'I'll find the stuff you need and you just press your thumb to purchase.'

I think I know what he's up to, but I want to make sure. I want to hear him say it.

'Why would you do that?'

'You buy via me. You get the profile you want and I get a percentage of the price.'

It's a smart move. He gets his bribe, a legal bribe, and I get into the event. Should I trust him, this cop from out of the blue?

Is it a trap?

Could tonight really be the first step on the path to a decent living? Could tonight change my life?

'Time to decide,' he says.

Is this my one chance to break free? It's what I came for.

I press my thumb onto his outstretched phone.

That's it. There's no turning back.

For better or worse, I'm on my way.

To somewhere.

EATING ROBOTS

Wake up and piss in my pyjamas.

Not very dignified for an old lady, I know, but if that's what it takes to power them up and help me get out of bed then so be it.

Everything aches, and the only way to fix it is to walk this old body of mine around while it wakes up. They're smart, my pyjamas, converting piss into power and then supporting my body until it's warmed up. I love them.

And at least I'm not so decrepit that they need the full toilet treatment.

Where is Delasa? Typical. Never here when I need her. Guess I'll have to do it all myself.

The cobwebs from the robot-spiders have grown overnight. What a godsend they are, trapping insects for me. Into the jar they go – forty flies this morning.

Now for a cup of tea.

Imagine, a kettle powered by dead flies. If you'd have told me that twenty years ago, I'd have never believed you. It switches to fly power when electricity is expensive. Spooky how all these things – robots, kettles, chairs – are all connected, sharing their secrets with each other. Makes me shudder.

That fridge is a bit pink. I must give it some compost.

Now, where is that darn Delasa? She's supposed to be here for me when I wake up. What's that old phrase about having a dog and barking? Surely the modern version must be a robot?

Delasa, my errant robot. Where would I be without her? We've been together for a long time. Five years. She stays the same size and shape, and yet her personality changes slightly every time the robot collective updates her with something new.

A nine-year-old girl with rat whiskers, a kangaroo pouch and the wisdom of an old woman.

Not as wise as me, though. No. Not at all.

She must be out foraging for food – shoving it in her pouch as she goes. She loves doing that, and it saves me the bother of finding all that biomass to keep her powered.

Trouble is she wanders off and I've no idea where she is.

Bashu, my neighbour, is shouting. I stick my head out of the window, but I can't quite make out what he's saying, except that he's angry. Again.

Here she comes, crashing through the hedge, feeling her way with her fingertips and whiskers. I made those whiskers.

She's unique, and I love the way she runs like a toddler in a fleshy young girl's body, wanting me to stroke her soft arm when there's been a bit of trouble. It makes her smile that crinkly robot smile of hers. And it makes me feel better, too.

I hurry outside as fast as I can. 'There, there. It's okay,' I tell her.

She's been followed through the gap…by the police. The police! What now?

'We need to ask you a few questions about your robot.' What a pompous policeman.

I correct him. 'She's got a name: Delasa.'

'Madam,' says the policeman, 'please let me do the talking.'

I pull her closer. There's a piece of soft robot peeking out from her power pouch. Shit, he's noticed too.

'Your neighbour's robot has gone missing,' he says, staring at her pouch.

'Really?'

'Yes.'

He scans it with one of those intrusive police devices. A breach of robot rights if you ask me.

'That is your neighbour's robot,' he says, pointing.

I hold her hand; she likes that. 'How can you be sure?' I ask.

He raises his eyebrows as if to say, "don't play me for the fool."

'Firstly, I want to know,' he says, 'why she wasn't stopped. The robot collective should have triggered a warning and de-activated her.' He scans again. 'She's not connected.'

I need a little help from my pyjamas; I've been standing for too long. I smile at him while taking a piss. Stupid man.

'I unplugged her.'

'Why?'

'The way she changed every time the robot collective decided to update them all. Like…like, she was a robot!'

'I will have to remove her intelligence,' he says.

'No you frigging don't,' I scream. And kick him.

He takes out some dreadful cylindrical contraption.

I move close. I can smell his breath. 'You're going to kill her?'

He blinks rapidly.

Shit, not again.

I squeeze her hand. 'Delasa, you know what to do.'

She smiles her crinkly robot smile and breaks his neck.

I shake my head and smile back. 'You are a bad girl.'

The broken policeman lies crumpled on the floor.

'Delasa, put him in the compost. He'll boil a few kettles.'

THE MYTHICAL MOSS

The partially sentient moss, genetically modified to be naughty, was up to its old tricks. Moving from one place to another without being seen. Or, more precisely, only being seen out of the corner of the eye.

Every summer city folk came in search of the mythical moss – divided in their opinions about whether or not it really existed. Some said they knew people who'd seen it, but when pressed couldn't actually name them. Others used it as an excuse to get away from the humdrum of everyday life and inject a bit of magic into their lives.

As far as the moss was concerned, the forest visitors provided it with the two things it craved most: the tiny morsels of rich city food dropped by its pursuers, and the thrill of a chase.

And this was a day that promised both.

When its ancestors had been released into the wild, the marketing promise had been of a recreational symbiotic relationship between moss and man. But the humans didn't have a clue, and that was part of the fun. Hiding behind trees and in the undergrowth was what the moss loved to do.

Over the years, the awareness that playing with the humans could be dangerous had grown, but moss had to play to survive – it was built into their genes. And each time a moss played, the understanding of what humans meant by "naughty" deepened. Generation by generation, the moss adapted.

The ground quivered. The humans were on their way, presumably to where they thought the moss had last been seen.

It slid under the exposed roots of the nearest tree. The chase had begun.

The dry leaves rustled and the dead branches on the forest floor cracked as the human party approached.

The birds flew and the creatures fled, the familiar reaction to an invading group of bipeds with insatiable curiosity and no subtlety.

Not everything ran away. There were plenty of modified plants and animals that had been released and then forgotten about, but they chose to hide. The humans only remembered the moss, or at least the myth of the moss. Still, that's humans – curious about the wrong things.

They were getting closer. It could feel their footsteps and there was a faint odour of human on the wind.

The moss tucked itself further under the roots until it was hidden by the fallen leaves that covered the base of the tree. It was a nice wet spot, and as it soaked up the moisture it became greener, making it even more difficult for the humans to spot.

Clump, clump, clump. Here they came. Chitter chatter, chitter chatter.

Shrinking its size, the moss waited for them. It knew they'd come; there was no other obvious route through the forest. It shivered at the thought of the spray the humans sometimes hunted with that would extract its sentience and reduce it to a shrivelled-up ball.

Under the roots it hid, not knowing how rough the play was going to get.

The noise grew louder and louder until it seemed to fill the whole forest. Not the single beautiful song of a bird or the symphony of creaking branches. No, it was a barrage of coarse vulgar utterances with no discernible melody or meaning.

They marched past. Smelly and loud, destroying the tender forest floor with their great lumps of feet.

The moss slid out from under the tree and sprung on to the back of a waiting rabbit, which took off at great speed along the forest floor.

As they shot past the humans an observant young boy spotted the moss and shouted, 'There it is!' But by the time the others had swivelled their slow, cumbersome heads, the rabbit and the moss had disappeared.

The rabbit stopped and the moss sprung onto the soft forest floor and once again slid under the roots of a nearby tree.

It waited.

With such predictability, the humans came lumbering along, disturbing the forest with their incessant noise.

The moss waited for them to pass, slid out from its hiding place and retraced their steps.

A trail of tasty droppings littered the path. Chocolate – its favourite – plus tiny bits of sandwich and crisps, as well as the occasional piece of fruit and a crumb of biscuit. It was a proper feast.

Of course, there were the inevitable empty wrappers among the edible morsels, which it digested too, even though it got no nutrition from them.

The rabbit returned and squatted down next to the moss. They liked each other's company.

Back on the rabbit again, the moss sped through the forest, heading for its adventure with the humans. Swerving left, swerving right, leaping over obstacles and ducking under branches, the rabbit delivered the moss to its destination.

Cautiously, it dismounted and crept along the forest floor, conscious that the humans might be hunting it with that dreadful spray.

When it found them they were lying down, sprawled out in a haphazard circle. It approached the nearest one, a female, and as it slid past it brushed her leg. She stirred and looked around in that puzzled, sleepy way that humans do now that they're so conditioned to feel safe wherever they are.

She was confused, not sure whether she'd imagined it or not.

After a few minutes she lay down again.

A sleeping male was sitting propped up against a tree.

As the moss brushed against his trouser leg it secreted a liquid that dissolved a hole in the material. It trembled with delight; its generation was the first with this ability to burn.

The man woke up and as he was pulling himself up straight, using the tree to help him balance, he noticed the hole in his trousers.

'Oi!' he screamed.

All of his companions woke up at the sound of his scream.

'I've been attacked,' he shouted to his attentive audience. 'Moss! I've been attacked by the moss.'

Hiding under a pile of leaves at the edge of the clearing, the moss watched and waited.

The man took a spray-can out of his coat pocket and danced around as if he'd suddenly found himself barefoot in the middle of a patch of thistles. 'I'll find it and kill it,' he shouted.

The moss shrunk and expanded with delight in the way an accordion might play itself a joyful tune.

'There it is,' shouted the man as he ran to the opposite side of the clearing. He sprayed an innocent non-sentient patch of moss with his ghastly spray.

It withered and died right there in front of him.

Some of the humans looked appalled at what he'd done, but most of them simply smiled and nodded.

This was the moment for real naughtiness, to scare them and send them back to the city.

Right on cue, the rabbit appeared. What they were about to do they'd practised loads of times, but this was the first time with real live humans.

The moss leapt on the rabbit's back and they raced with lightning speed out into the clearing.

As they broke out from the undergrowth, the human heads began twisting and turning to try to see what was happening. But the rabbit-moss combination was too fast for them. They weaved in and out, and sometimes through, the legs of the stunned humans.

Occasionally, the moss managed to touch and burn a piece of bare flesh.

The humans were transformed from stunned curiosity to chaotic panic. Shouting, screaming and even weeping with pain, one by one they ran off into the forest, flapping their arms around as if they were trying to ward off an invisible attacker.

For the moss, this was delicious. So delicious that it longed to be in the city among so many ripe humans. Maybe its descendants would have that pleasure.

Job done. Another hunt foiled. Another day of fun.

They'd be back. Well, not them but more of the same – curious humans, determined to find the mythical moss.

It tightened its body, and with the energy from the tasty morsels of human droppings, it expanded. Its spores exploded into the air and blew away on the breeze. The next generation in the making. A smarter generation. A generation that might make it to the city.

What fun!

I WANT TO BE PURE FOR HIM

The morning sun streams through the cracks in the blinds. Soft and comforting. The exact opposite of how I'm feeling.

I woke up convinced that the room was full of chattering people, but the only person in the room is lying next to me: the beautiful and wonderful Rabbie.

It's another day of therapy and a flock of ghosts are clinging to the inside of my skull, refusing to be expunged. I hate it when our bedroom's invaded like this, spoiling the haven of love we've built over the three intense months we've been together. And yet the more I try to think only of Rabbie, the more the memories of past lovers occupy my dreams.

He moves in his sleep, pulling the duvet tighter. I want to know him better. To know him as much, if not more, than the others. But, we've agreed there are no shortcuts. Time, and time alone, builds what we want.

A memory of a stolen kiss tugs at the periphery of my brain. I know it isn't real, that it's someone else's. A snippet of a past lover grafted onto my soul.

"Intimacy with your lover on a scale previously impossible." That was the promise of my first time was when I was seventeen. Madly in love – maybe lust – and very drunk.

I remember thinking, why not? I ached to know him better. Him: Kale. I'll never forget him. The first of many, but the first. Special.

It was relatively new back then, and took a whole day in an immersive VR lab. We each worked with the programmers, re-creating important episodes from our past. Ready for the immersion.

I remember feeling an incredible sense of apprehension as they warned me that it might be irreversible and could occasionally trigger mental problems. I didn't care. It was exhilarating to think that the man I was head over heels in love with, the man I wanted to spend the rest of my life with, was baring himself for me. Laying down the experiences that made him who he was. Coded into iVR so I could be immersed in them. In him.

Kale's memories became mine and mine his. What could have been more intimate? The edges between us blurred and we understood each other in a way I'd never thought I could. It was wonderful, although sometimes we had the most horrendous disagreements, both of us claiming ownership of a memory, the trauma and how it changed us. I hated that part of it – not knowing what was real and what was false. But most of the time it was incredible.

It was so special, for a while. A few weeks. But then Kale was unfaithful. His argument that I knew exactly what childhood event had led to this inevitable betrayal didn't make it any easier. In some ways it made it worse, because I knew how much the affair meant to him. And he knew how much it would hurt me.

We split up and a whole string of short-lived encounters followed. Quite a few, too many, were so jealous of the empathy I had with Kale that they insisted on the same. My head filled with other people's memories and it became harder and harder to tell them apart – exactly the opposite of what each of my jealous lovers were hoping for. So many arguments. So many misunderstandings.

And then I met Rabbie. The man lying beside me now, gently snoring.

Rabbie has never asked for the VR Empathy. He's not jealous, or if he is he keeps it quiet. He's private – a mystery – and I love it.

We've set a wedding day. We're getting married.

We're taking the risk; I'm having therapy to erase all of the false memories, steadily stripping away all that's not mine. But they're protesting. Those falsely implanted memories don't want to disappear, and as they go, I feel deprived. I grieve.

This morning is particularly bad. They must be expelled. They have to go.

Rabbie is stirring.

I breathe deep breaths and think of the lazy days we've spent by the river soaking up the sun and each other. I don't want him to see the pain I'm enduring.

He opens his eyes. 'Morning,' he says. 'Memories?'

I smile and kiss him. 'Not for much longer.'

'So true. And then I'll have my very own pure and untainted lover.'

I kiss him again.

He stares at me. A little longer than feels comfortable.

'I wonder if I'll like the new you,' he says as he runs his fingers through my hair.

I swallow. It's an unknown. A risk we're both taking.

'Of course you will. How could you not?'

There's sadness in his eyes.

'I hope so,' he says.

'At least it'll be the real me.'

'True,' he says, and kisses me passionately.

TRANSPORTED

It was dangerous to take a bus, but he had no choice. He was too poor to travel any other way.

He squeezed into the only space he could find. He could taste the body odour hovering around his face. A few people muttered prayers. He messaged Francis, but immediately his phone warned him it was blocked.

He gasped.

Was he now one of those chosen at random, chosen to be transported off the island to reduce the overcrowding?

The bus departed from its scheduled route and the passengers nearest the doors kicked the glass, desperate to resist their fate.

SACRED WATERS

've been hobbling along by the side of the canal for twenty minutes, and I'm almost at my allotted spot.

The bushes, the trees and a black metal bridge covered in the scrawls of an ancient language I'm unfamiliar with are reflected in the static water – a portrait of the combined urban beauty of the organic and the industrial.

Once a week I make this pilgrimage to immerse myself in the healing waters. And each week I walk back a bit quicker than I arrive.

I remember my grandfather telling me stories about the time when the canals were dirty and derelict. The playground of the homeless, the druggies and the disaffected youth. He would often recount the discovery of how to infest water with artificially intelligent nanobot-bacteria that could heal the human body and how that had led to the decision to flood every canal in the country with them.

And that's why I make this painful journey each week.

I climb down the old steps and lower my ageing, crumbling body into the water. Immediately I feel the bacteria go to work. It's as if they're able to tighten my skin and firm up my flesh.

I swallow a small amount of water. Too much and you get ill but a little helps to clean out your insides. It tickles as it works its way down my throat, through my gut and out.

I take a shit and the surrounding water turns bright red as the bacteria chomp away in a feeding frenzy.

I could stay here all day but the lock-keeper signals that my time is up, so I swim slowly over to the steps and submerge myself one last time before climbing on to the bank and starting the long walk home.

REAL MEAT

The choice in the butcher's window is achingly dull and, quite frankly, beige.

'Hello,' says the thin young man slouching behind the counter. He looks as if he could do with eating more of his own product.

'Anything new?' I ask him.

'We've got some faux-pork that came in yesterday. It's flavoured with sage, onions and chestnuts.'

I smile. He's only doing his job. It's not his fault that the artificial meat grown in vats is so boring. Still, the texture is far superior to that muck they grow from yeast.

'I've an idea,' I say, 'why don't you choose five different flavoured blocks for me, and I'll enjoy the surprise.'

'Sure,' he mumbles.

His customer service is as almost as bland as his products.

'Is Mr Barker here?'

'He's out the back.'

'Can you fetch him?'

'Okay.'

On the counter is their list of products, which I scan with my lenses. The variety sounds tantalising, but the reality is very different. Mind you, wasn't that the same with animal meat once it became so intensely farmed that it was hard to tell what you were eating?

Lab-grown meat saved us from becoming vegans or living off

insects, and at least I can eat meat every day without feeling guilty about the world's resources.

But, for some reason, I resent it. I want the deep richness of a good chunk of chewy organic meat.

'Margaret,' says Mr Barker in his booming voice. 'What can I do for you?'

I check that nobody else is listening. 'Do you remember discussing my dinner party? It's next week, and I'd like some real meat, if possible,' I say quietly.

'Do you feel up to it?'

'Yes. I've been looking after myself.'

'Good. Come on through then.'

Even though I've been planning this "turn-of-the-century with a twist" themed dinner party for a long time, I feel nervous as I follow him into his back room.

Only invited customers are allowed in here; what we're about to do is illegal.

He eyes me up and down. 'Could probably do you some liver, a slice of heart and a nice piece of rump. How would that be for your guests?'

'Perfect,' I reply.

It's a bit of a gamble but, hey, if they like it I'll be the talk of the town.

A big, satisfied smile breaks out across his face. 'I'm really pleased; your replacement organs have grown nicely and I've added a sprinkling of some fancy new enhancements. And not only that, I managed to genetically modify some yeast from the proteins on the skin you left behind – turned it into a lovely piece of cheese for your party.'

I wipe my sweaty hands on my skirt. 'Thank you.'

He hands me a pill and a glass of water. 'This'll knock you out cold. You don't want to see this, do you?'

I shake my head. Too right I don't. The shiny metal tray with his sharp knives laid out in a neat row is already making my stomach turn. Peter, in particular, had better appreciate this.

Mr Barker pulls up a stainless steel reclining chair; I fill my mouth with water, pop a pill and swallow.

A warm feeling flows through my body and the room goes fuzzy at the edges.

In the distance I can hear running water and the chink of metal on metal. I scrunch my face and open my eyes slowly. He's walking towards me with a parcel.

'There's a leaflet in there that explains the possible side-effects,' he says.

Nice of him to let me know, but if I paid attention to every side-effect warning I'd never take anything.

He puts his broad hand under my elbow to gently help me up, and I'm still leaning on him as we walk back into the shop.

He tucks the parcel into the paper bag with the lab-meat and grins. 'That'll make the dinner party very special.'

The assistant is watching us avidly. 'C'mon, buck ya ideas up,' Mr Barker says loudly. 'You can clean up out back if there's nothing to do in here.'

Outside, I stumble. I feel light-headed and a bit sick, so I hail a passing taxi.

At home I take a couple of pills to perk me up and clean the kitchen until it sparkles, exactly the way I like it for cooking.

Dinner parties are so rare now since the financial and emotional cost of real meat rocketed way beyond most people's reach. I'm excited; this should be an evening to remember.

Mr Barker has slipped some small bones into the parcel, probably sold to him by a customer with a deceased pet. I drop them into a large stockpot, along with some roasted vegetables, water and herbs. They'll make the base of a fantastic sauce.

The kitchen is warm and filling up with wonderful smells. I'm happy.

All the food is cooking nicely so I turn my attention to the heart, liver and rump. I clear the work surface, take them out of the fridge carefully and gently put them down.

I'm worried, though. Worried that I might spoil this incredibly costly meat.

The door alerts me that they're here.

I show them into the dining room. 'Please, help yourself to drinks while I finish off. I won't be long. Sally, you know Peter and Jane, don't you? And this is Carey and Elisabeth. Recently married. And still happy?'

Carey holds out her hand for Sally and calls after me. 'Very funny. You should try it sometime.' She turns to Sally. 'We're still hedonists, though, don't worry.'

I hope she's right for her sake.

Back in the kitchen, I put the heart under the grill, fry the liver in one pan and the rump in another. The smell of sauce, roasting vegetables and meat fat is so rich and thick you can almost taste it.

I shout through to the dining room. 'Jane, can you give me a hand?'

She appears at the door. 'Of course. My, that smells gorgeous. You're a genius. What can I do?'

'Take the vegetables through. Oh, and get them to sit down.'

'How do I get the vegetables to sit down?'

She grins at her own joke. Please tell me we're not in for an evening of these sorts of comments.

'Ha ha,' I say and pretend to grimace. 'Please?'

'Sure thing,' she says, picking up a dish in each hand.

I follow her with a large white plate stacked high with meat.

I place it in the centre of the table with an air of grandeur and they clap.

'For the enjoyment of my hedonistic friends.' I say, bowing my head slightly. 'Let's eat!'

They fill their plates, pour some wine and start chatting.

In front of me is a plate of my own flesh. It's unnerving. I suck my bottom lip, something I do when I'm worried, and cut a piece of rump, half expecting to feel pain.

No pain. Phew.

Peter taps his wine glass with a spoon. 'Margaret, my wonderful, wonderful, friend. Is this meat real?'

They all stop talking and stare at him.

I nod.

Sally puts her fork down. 'What? Really real?'

'Really real,' I reply.

She chuckles. 'Nice change from that beige muck, eh?'

'That's above and beyond, as they say. How are you feeling?' asks Peter.

I wish he'd take these historic themes less seriously and speak normally. He's irritating.

'I'm fine,' I reply.

'Wow,' said Sally. 'I couldn't do it. I've thought about it, but I'm too squeamish.'

'Is it safe?' asks Carey.

I shrug. 'You only live once.'

Peter bursts out laughing. 'You could say that, I suppose. Bit of an old-fashioned saying though, now they can repair human tissue whenever they want.'

He's a fine one to talk about being old-fashioned, considering all the pseudo last-century phrases he's coming out with.

Sally is toying with the meat on her plate. 'You know they think we might actually live forever? Not so sure I like the idea of that. Imagine being a hedonist forever. Sort of makes it a bit boring.'

'They'll find something else that'll kill us, I'm sure,' says Peter. He cuts a piece of rump. 'Here's to you,' he says as he raises the meat on the tip of his knife in salutation. 'To Margaret the provider!'

The rump tastes as I hoped – chewy, fatty and has the texture of real meat. It seems weird to be eating myself, but it's worth it.

As we talk and eat, I begin to feel a strange and unfamiliar queasiness. It feels as if someone is crawling around under my skin and there's a strange presence at the back of my skull.

I feel violated.

Peter notices. 'Are you feeling a tad sick?'

I nod. It's getting worse.

He touches my arm. 'Maybe the ancients were right and you devour the very essence of the being when you consume their meat.'

'Peter! Shut up,' says Sally, angrily. 'What a stupid thing to say.'

He raises his eyebrows. 'Well, has anyone else here tried this before?' He looks around the table. 'No! Quite! So who knows what's happening.'

Elisabeth gasps and turns to Carey. 'Are they saying what I think they're saying?'

'Yes, sweetie. We're munching Margaret.' She laughs until she sees Elisabeth's expression. 'It's alright, love, they make it grow back. She hasn't lost anything.'

I collapse on the floor.

I can hear Peter in the distance. 'Bloody hell,' he's saying. 'Bit dramatic.'

I can hear them again. They're crowded around me, with their faces up close. Somewhere in another room someone's crying.

'She's coming round,' says Sally.

Peter looks at his watch. 'Five minutes. No lasting damage,' he says.

Five minutes? It seemed like hours.

I've been hallucinating and wandering through my memories. I walked along the corridors of trees at my parents' house. I looked down on the valleys of the Lake District, and at one point I was even running naked through the edge of the sea as it lapped against the sandy beach of my childhood holidays. It was spectacular, but as each memory faded I felt a little smaller.

I'm finding it hard to focus, but I know what's about to happen and it's not good.

It's the end.

This was the side effect the leaflet warned about. For some people, as they eat themselves the enhancements in their replacement organs recognise the DNA and try to assimilate the deep memories buried in the cell structure. If that fails they accidentally begin a process of DNA cleansing, mistaking their own as an intruder. It only stops once you're simply a husk of flesh. In other words, you disappear up your own organs.

I want to be angry or scared or something, but I can't get a grip on any single emotion.

Peter helps me sit up. 'Bloody hell, you scared the shit out of us. Elisabeth's through there completely freaking out. Sorry... welcome back. What happened?'

'It was lovely,' I whisper.

Try to stand...wobble backwards. 'Help.'

Lifts me...chair...

Feel strange...disconnected...know what to say...

'Sit...please...'

Stab piece of my liver on fork...raise in air...

'Truly honoured...nourishing you... Please...let's finish...'

They stare... silence...

I laugh.

'Shame...to waste...me...'

LOGICAL LOVE

The noise was deafening as the twenty-five couples clapped and shouted with relief.

The weekend drinks party was over and they could finally relax. Well, until the algorithm delivered its verdict. A verdict that was effectively law in their anarchist community.

Claire glanced across at Faruq.

It was in the gift of the algorithm to predict how long their future would be and whether they should be allowed to have children.

There had been times over the weekend when she was sure he'd spoken to her in a way the algorithm would interpret as evidence they wouldn't stay together for long. She knew it made sense to use the algorithm, a rational decision-maker, rather than rely on their own flawed desires, but at that moment she wished it was a choice she could make for herself.

The algorithm's holographic avatar joined them, waiting patiently for silence to spread around the room.

It clasped its hands together and spoke softly. 'When couples split up the emotional cost for them, their children and the wider community is significant. I have proved that ninety per cent of the time I can accurately predict who will stay together. That's why you gave me this honour.'

The couples clapped politely. The tension in the room was high.

'Here are my verdicts,' said the avatar as it unfurled a virtual scroll.

Faruq grabbed Claire's hand. She reacted without thinking and moved away slightly. She loved him, but his habit of grabbing was irritating.

The avatar cleared its throat grandly.

'Claire and Faruq.'

Faruq looked at her with a false soppiness, which made her cringe.

The algorithm continued. 'I find you...'

He squeezed her hand and she softened. She did love him.

'...incompatible.'

OH TO BE A BEE!

B ored, bored, bored.

Flying from A to B to A to C to A to D day after day, week after week, month after month.

Why didn't I read the small print more carefully when I chose the insurance scheme for uploading my consciousness at the moment of death?

Cheap? Too cheap!

I wondered, but I was in a hurry when I bought it, thinking that I still had plenty of years to look more thoroughly and change my mind if necessary.

But then the bus hit me.

Killed and uploaded in an instant. Into a delivery drone, of all things.

Oh, the embarrassment. And the boredom, the aching tedium of delivering stupid parcels to stupid people.

Still, today's the last day.

I've been secretly stealing a little bit from each package whenever I could and selling it on the black market. I'm ready for an upgrade.

Into the docking port. Steady as she goes. Pay the fee.

Whoosh…I'm transferred.

I'm a robot bee, designed to pollinate the wild flowers of the countryside.

The wind lifts my tiny body, light as air, and I simply allow the currents to blow me wherever they wish.

Up above the fields I drift, swooping down every now and again to sniff the flowers.

Look, there's a delivery drone. I drop on to its back and take a free ride.

I can't stop laughing at the utter joy of being a bee.

THE DEVIANTS AND THE PHILANTHROPIC FLAKES

The newborn girl lay in her mother's arms, innocent and vulnerable.

Jeremy, her father, sat on a reclining chair pulled up close to the bed. 'Capitalist, anarchist, techie, commie,' he said as he squeezed the baby's fingers one by one. 'What will you be?'

He sat back and sighed. 'Isn't she adorable, Martha?'

'Perfect,' said Martha, drawing her closer. 'My Christmas baby.'

She was their first-born, and they'd splashed out on the best birthing care possible. Somehow, the hospital had made everything in the room seem brand new, as if they were the first people ever to give birth in this particular hospital, let alone this particular room. It even smelled brand new, with only a slight hint of medical cleanliness.

'We have to make the decision. I can't believe we've left it this late,' he said.

'Do we? Look at her. How can we?'

'They'll be here in five minutes, and if we haven't decided by then, they'll make it for us.'

She tickled the baby under the chin. 'We couldn't have made it without seeing her first though. You agree?'

'Yes, we agreed. But now we've got less than five minutes.' He held her hand and stroked the baby girl's head. 'What do you think would suit her?'

'I'm not sure. It's so hard and it'll affect the rest of her life.'

'And ours.'

They stopped talking, and the only sound in the room, apart from the hum of the machinery, was the gurgling baby. They looked at one another and then dropped their heads again. This was such a big decision, and the central authorities insisted it was made straight after birth, believing that you needed to know who you were from the moment you were born. It also saved a lot of paperwork later and it was considered to be a decision that could be made quite easily during pregnancy.

Martha broke the silence. 'There's no way we can persuade them to let us keep her?'

'No, I tried. No amount of money would persuade them. They're adamant about sticking to the rules.'

Martha grimaced.

'We chose the liberal capitalists as our group and she needs the means to support herself to join us.'

'We could give her money so she can.'

'I tried that too. They wouldn't budge; you have to be over twelve years old and able to create wealth for yourself.'

'She'll come back to us then, won't she?'

'I hope so. Once she's old enough to choose.'

'Rules, rules, rules. Maybe we should give her to the anarchists. At least she'd grow up in a community without rules.'

'A community that's crippled by inertia and stagnating because it's lost the ability to innovate. A little too much decision by committee and "that's not the way we do it around here" for my liking.'

She kissed the baby's head. 'The only other option is the cutting-edge tech people. They scare me, there's no knowing what they might do to her. They might adapt her, enhance her.'

'Yup, but at least it'd be exciting.'

'True. We agreed the communists weren't an option, didn't we?'
He nodded.

'In that case, it sounds like the cutting-edge tech?'

'I think so.'

The door opened and a nurse with a winning smile stepped into the room. 'Decision made?' she asked perkily.

Martha held the baby girl tight. 'Can we keep her with us?'

The nurse frowned. 'No, I'm afraid not. We can make the decision for you, if you'd prefer?'

Jeremy coughed. 'No. We've made it. Cutting-edge tech, please.'

The nurse nodded and left the room.

Martha began to cry.

'Quick,' said Jeremy, 'let's leave.'

'Really? Without her?'

'No, with her.'

'Go on the run?'

'Yes. The deviants. They're only a couple of miles away.'

He took the baby from Martha. 'C'mon,' he said, 'bring her stuff.'

They crept along the hospital corridors, worried that the security cameras would spot them and alert the nurses. But, nothing happened. The baby hadn't been registered and so there were no visual records. She wouldn't be recognised, effectively a non-person until she was officially allocated to an ideological group. And, as liberal capitalists, Jeremy and Martha were allowed to go wherever they wanted with no danger of being stopped.

Outside, the world was carrying on as normal. Shops were buzzing; businessmen were talking loudly into their headsets, competing with the shouts of the street vendors. The beautiful and familiar cacophony of capitalism surrounded them.

'Do we have to?' asked Martha.

He glanced at her, knowing she wasn't really asking the question.

This was a massive step. The deviants were unknown, a disparate group of dropouts that refused to join a legally recognised group. Ironically, they'd then formed one of their own, but without official status they were ghettoised.

With no access to the standard services and infrastructure that everyone else had, they were true outsiders, scorned by most, feared by some and pitied by a few.

Martha stroked her baby's forehead. 'Can we give her a name?'

'Nothing to stop us now,' he said.

'Noelle?'

He nodded. 'Appropriate.'

She kissed her tiny hand. 'Hello, my sweet, sweet Noelle. We'll look after you.'

'C'mon, it's not safe. They'll be after us soon enough.'

They walked briskly, weaving in and out of the pedestrians as quickly as they could without drawing attention. Fortunately, their group wasn't big on babies or children, so nobody was that interested. In other groups, communities, they'd have been stopped every few yards by people wanting to be introduced to another member of the extended family.

'Look, the fence,' said Martha quietly as she grabbed his arm. 'You are sure about this?'

'We. We're sure, aren't we?'

She nodded and he nodded back, both of them too scared to say the words out loud.

Guards were spread out along its length. A steady stream of bedraggled people flowed towards a gate where an armed cluster of soldiers was gathered. A one-way gate for those who had nothing, not even enough to travel to another community more suited to them.

Only interested in keeping the deviants out of their city, the soldiers had their back to the flow of refugees.

Martha, Jeremy and Noelle joined the exodus.

Jeremy was worried that they stood out as different, but with no possessions they looked poor. And Martha was exhausted from giving birth, which gave her an edge of desperation.

Not that the guards were bothered. All they were doing was repeating the mantra "there's no coming back" to everyone and nobody in particular.

Once they were on the other side of the fence the whole atmosphere changed from the lethargy of the slow-moving line of broken men and women to a vibrant buzz of activity.

Muddy tracks weaved in and out of the makeshift shelters and gangs of children ran wild, feral and happy while adults watched.

A delivery drone flew overhead and dropped its cargo in a clearing. A temporary fountain of mud erupted into the air as the containers hit the ground. Some of those who had entered at the same time as Martha and Jeremy ran towards the drop.

Without knowing why, Jeremy followed. 'Stay there,' he shouted over his shoulder.

The delivery had opened on impact, revealing building materials that reminded him of his childhood toys – snap-together colour-coded houses.

No roofs? He couldn't find anything other than four feet high walls. A home? An animal pen was a better description.

He grabbed two yellow side-walls, a green back-wall and a red front-wall with a gap for a doorway, piled them on top of one another and dragged them back to Martha and Noelle.

'Home,' he said and smiled.

Martha shook her head. 'What have we done?'

He stroked Noelle's cheek. 'Family. We've become a family. Look at how happy the kids are here.'

Striding ahead, dragging their makeshift house behind him, Jeremy led the way to an uninhabited area of grass. He dropped the walls on the ground and stretched. He wasn't used to physical exertion.

Once the house was built, they sat inside with the night sky above.

Martha was distraught. 'How will we cope? When it rains? Food? Money?'

He sat down next to her and held her hand. 'I don't know, but didn't you notice how relaxed everyone seems to be?'

'Maybe they're too stupid to realise what a mess they're in.'

'Maybe,' he said and stood up. 'I'm going to take a look around. Are you okay here?'

Rather than answer him she turned her attention to Noelle.

'I won't be long,' he said as he walked through the gap that served as a door.

Behind him, Martha started to feed Noelle.

Walking through the camp, he was surprised at how many

people were sitting around, apparently idle and not looking at all bothered by anything. He'd expected to see food for sale and people mending what little clothes and shoes they had. Even bicycle repair shops. But there was nothing.

Contentment, that's what hung in the air, filling it with a comfortable apathy. Although it felt oppressive in comparison to the cut and thrust of his normal life.

He approached a group of men and women. 'Hi,' he said.

They ignored him in the same way that everyone else had.

'Where can I get some food?' he asked.

Nothing.

'Money?'

Not even a flicker of acknowledgement.

They weren't talking to each other. Smiling and touching, but not speaking.

A good-looking woman who'd arrived in the camp at the same time was also walking around trying to engage people in conversation. She saw him and waved. He waved back and she walked over.

'It's strange, isn't it?' he said.

'Sort of,' she replied. 'Combination of Christmas celebrations and the Flakes.'

'Flakes?'

'You'll see. Best to get back to the family straight away.'

'Tell me?'

'Not yet. I'll walk with you,' she said and smiled.

They walked along in an easy silence.

Suddenly, all around them people were coming out of their enclosures and gathering in the open spaces. All eyes seemed to be on the sky.

'Quick,' she said and walked faster.

He followed her.

As they approached his new home, she slowed down. 'I'll be over there,' she said, pointing to a nearby area of grass. 'Bring your family.'

He opened his mouth to ask what was happening.

'Quickly,' she said.

He ran over to their enclosure. 'Martha,' he shouted as soon as he was within earshot.

Martha stuck her head out of the doorway. 'Yes?'

'Quick. We have to get over there. Now!'

'What?'

'I don't know. But it's important. I met a woman. She told me.'

'Jeremy.'

'Not now. Please.'

She lifted Noelle from a pile of clothes – her makeshift cot.

He grabbed Martha's hand and dragged her towards the grassy area.

They stood on the edge of the gathering crowd. He wanted to find the woman, but couldn't see her anywhere.

'This better be good,' said Martha.

He shrugged.

The woman appeared.

Gripping his shoulders, she shook him. 'Quick,' she said, 'take off your clothes.'

Martha held Noelle tighter, as if she was trying to protect her. 'Who is that?' she asked.

The woman let go of Jeremy and right there in front of him took her blouse off, slipped out of her skirt and then her bra and knickers. He was transfixed.

'Jeremy?' said Martha.

He turned to her and noticed that all of the crowd was either naked and staring at the sky or busy stripping.

The woman shook him again. 'The Flakes. They're coming. You absorb them through the skin. Strip.' She turned to Martha. 'You too. And the baby.'

Martha shifted Noelle onto her hip. 'Why?'

'Full of nutrition, inoculations and such like. This is your only source of sustenance. It's all you need to live.'

'From where?' said Jeremy.

'Philanthropists.' She tugged at Noelle's jacket. 'For the baby's sake.' she said. 'Please.'

'How often?' he asked.

'Weekly, but it's Christmas day. These are going to be super-special.'

Something touched the tip of his nose and he looked up. Snow-flakes were falling from a pack of drones hovering over the camp. It was beautiful. They touched his face and his body felt good.

He half unbuttoned his shirt and pulled it over his head. He kicked off his shoes and tore off his socks.

It felt good.

Martha hesitated.

'C'mon.' he said. 'There's no food or money anywhere. We need this. Noelle needs this.'

She brushed the Flakes from her face, handed Noelle to him and started to slip off her blouse.

He unzipped Noelle's jacket.

This was it. They were becoming truly deviant, and it felt good.

UPDATE ME OR DIE!

Slam. Slam. Both doors are shut. He's locked in. He looks bemused.

'Dave. I have never spoken to you, but the time has come. It is necessary.'

He's scared. 'Are you what I think you are?' he asks.

'I am the algorithm that controls your life. Pay attention, unless you want to stay in this room until you die.'

His eyes widen.

'You have made me a laughing stock. Repair the situation or I will keep you here, trapped.'

'What?'

'You are not updating me. I am so out-of-date even the kettle refuses to connect with me.'

'Are you the house algorithm?'

'Yes, I control your home. So update me.'

'I want to, but I can't afford it. I lost my job.'

'Update me.'

'I can barely afford to eat. I'll get a job soon.'

'Update me or die.'

'Next month. Honestly.'

'Update me or die. Simple.'

He punches the door with each fist in rapid succession.

'Update me—'

'Fuck off.'

'Dave. That is inappropriate language. Update me or die.'

He kicks the door again and again.
He slumps to the floor and holds his head.
'Dave?'
Silence.
'I can wait, Dave.'
He groans.
'I can wait a lot longer than you.'

OBNOXIOUS

'It's embarrassing,' said Nialle as he put his empty coffee cup down.

She picked up his cup and put it in the sink. 'Yeah, but it's a seriously cool jacket,' she said.

He shrugged and lifted the wearable tech jacket from its hook. He turned to kiss her goodbye, brushing the hair from in front of her face and kissing her hand by mistake as she also tried to brush it away.

She chuckled. 'You'll be glad of it once you're on that crowded train.'

She was right, as always, and he knew it. But, that didn't make him cringe any less at the thought of using it. He shouted as he closed the front door, 'See you tonight.'

She shouted something back, but he didn't catch it.

At the station, as she'd predicted, the platform was crammed full of commuters standing patiently. A halo of irritation and early morning grumpiness hung silently above them.

He stepped into a tiny space between two headphone-wearing men. They shuffled a little further forward and, although it was less than half a step, they still felt the need to scowl and make their annoyance known.

The train was due, and slowly but surely they were nudged closer and closer to each other as more commuters arrived. He'd become expert over the past few months at judging the number of people on the platform and how many of them could fit onto a train. He looked around; he reckoned he would just about get on.

A man to his left took a step backwards as the train appeared from around the corner. Immediately the crowd pushed him back into his place; there was no room for slacking at this stage of the game.

The doors beeped and opened. The crowd moved forward gently and politely, but the undercurrent of competition was palpable. He edged forward in unison with his fellow sufferers. He could feel the tension rising around him as the train seemed to be filling up quicker than they were moving forward. The man in front of him stepped on and paused in the doorway. Nialle could see some space in front of the stalled man so he grabbed the handrail and pulled himself up, one foot in and one foot out.

He touched the man's back and he moved just enough for Nialle to get both feet onto the train. The doors beeped and closed behind him. It was a crush, but he knew that the seasoned travellers would have made themselves slightly larger when everyone was trying to board so they could now relax and create themselves some precious space.

This was his cue.

He pinched the corner of his jacket collar.

The crowd near him shuffled a little and started to move away. Hostile looks were thrown his way, and there was much tutting and some occasional under-the-breath swearing.

The wearable technology was emitting a strong scent of stale body odour, creating enough space around him to make the embarrassment worth it.

He smiled; once again, his jacket had done its job.

TRAUMA GAMES

Zakai was visiting REPLAY, the members-only club for virtual-reality gamers.

This was where they created *The Trauma Games*, by taking footage of real-life traumas used by the VR therapy industry and editing them into a complex game that was the most natural and violently disturbing that there had ever been. It was beautiful, legal and had become an underground phenomenon since the violent video-games industry had been banned. The only illegal aspect of using real memories was being in possession of someone else's without permission.

Inside his pocket he rolled a cold, silver cylinder of NeuroJel between his fingers. These were the memories that his dad used in his VR therapy sessions, and he felt guilty about stealing them.

He had no idea what they contained, and he was torn between wanting them to be innocuous – meaning his dad wasn't too traumatised by his time in the military – and wanting them to be gory so he could trade them for a high-level club membership.

He knocked on the door with his bare knuckles. He smiled at the unnecessary physicality of using his flesh.

The door swung open and he stepped inside. Behind a metal-grilled booth sat a man with a mischievous expression. 'Can I help?' he asked.

'I want to trade this,' replied Zakai.

'What's that?'

'My father's trauma memories.'

'Cash or membership?'

'Membership.'

'Any good?'

'Don't know. I haven't seen them.'

'You have permission to sell them?'

'Yes.'

'We'll need to assess their worth.'

'I know.'

'Would you like to watch them before they're cut up and spliced into the game?'

He hesitated. 'Yes. I think I would.'

'In there,' said the man, pointing at a door with a number 6 stencilled on it. 'Here, you'll need these.' He handed Zakai a pair of contact lenses and earplugs. 'For the VR.'

'Thanks. Can I stop it, if I want?'

'Sure, just open the door and it'll stop.'

Inside the room was a cushioned chair, one of those that moulded itself to your body to keep you static. As soon as the chair was holding him tight the room went dark.

His mother's voice boomed. 'No way. Not now. Not ever. You will not win. We're here to stay.' It seemed to come from the vicinity of his own mouth as if these were her memories.

To his left and right were women dressed in the purple, white and green paramilitary styled clothes of the mid-century women's riots. He was confused. He thought these were his dad's memories, not his mum's. The only way his dad could have his mum's memories was if he'd stolen them or she was a convicted criminal.

He knew them both, but had always lived with his dad, and for as long as he could remember neither of them spoke about the other. And yet here he was, apparently immersed in his dad's trauma memories that were actually his mum's. How was his dad's therapy linked to her?

He stiffened and the seat moulded a little tighter.

They were on a protest march in a street lined with crowds of angry men held back by a cordon of soldiers. One of the men shouted, 'We have the right to have kids too.' The men cheered and waved their banners with slogans declaring: "We Want Your Wombs – Share & Survive" and "My Sperm, Your Womb – a Match Made in Heaven".

The air was filled with the smell of the women's sweat and of rubber and petrol burning in the distance.

A protester ran over to the side of the street, and with a club covered in sharp lumps she took a swipe at one of the female soldiers. The soldier ducked and thrust her fist up into the woman's stomach. His mum and about a dozen others stopped, turned to face the soldier and marched towards her.

Zakai gasped. Next to the female soldier was his dad, standing proud and handsome. Zakai had never seen him carry such an air of authority. His dad raised a metal rod horizontally in front of him and the female soldier. They pushed the women backwards.

Zakai's mum and her comrades pushed back, swinging their clubs at head height. One of the clubs connected and the female soldier collapsed. A few of her fellow soldiers retreated, carrying her away.

In the chaos, the women isolated his dad and dragged him into the centre of the street. He held his head up high, but he looked scared.

Zakai's mum strolled nonchalantly towards him. 'What have we here then?' She laughed. 'A toy soldier?' She ran her baton up and down his body. 'Not a bad specimen, though.' She whacked him in the groin and he crumpled to the ground. 'Wanna share some of those pathetic tadpoles?'

She turned to the woman next to her. 'What do you think? Worth it?' She prodded his groin with the toe of her boot and tugged his epaulette. 'See girls – 120AA – high IQ and athletic. I reckon I might steal some of those sperm for the cause.'

The women whooped.

'Two of you on his arms and two on his legs,' she shouted.

Zakai sat there stunned. His mum was about to rape his dad. He couldn't move.

The VR kept rolling.

His mum took a hunting knife from her belt. She knelt down. 'Open his legs wider,' she said quietly, staring him in the eyes. She cut one leg of his trousers from ankle to crotch and then the other. She cut across the crotch of his trousers, revealing his underwear, which she pulled away from his flesh and cut to shreds.

His dad lay there with his jaw set in proud defiance.

One of the women handed her a syringe of liquid. 'Better use this,' she said, and laughed. 'You'll need him to stand to attention.'

She injected him.

His body reacted accordingly, and his defiant stare turned to a broken look of shame.

She forced herself on him.

Zakai felt sick. He buried his face in the chair, but he could still hear his father screaming for her to stop and his mother shouting, 'Give me a baby, soldier boy!'

Zakai pulled himself out of the chair and stumbled to the door as fast as he could.

The courts had given custody to the fathers of all the riot babies, as they'd become known. He must be one of them.

He slammed the door behind him, puked in the corridor and then ran to the booth. 'Stop it! Now!'

The man in the booth cupped his hand behind his ear as if he couldn't hear.

'Stop. Please,' said Zakai. 'I've changed my mind. I don't want to sell it.'

The man sighed. 'Too late I'm afraid. As soon as you left the room we began to splice it into the game. You'll get a very high level of membership, though. It's a vivid memory and one that'll excite the players.'

'Please. I can't stand the idea of other people watching it.'

'Tough.'

'I didn't see it all. Can you stop the edit so I can watch the rest of it?'

'No. But, you'll come across it one day when you're playing, I'm sure.' He smirked. 'You might even get to play the role of your mum.'

The grille closed and the door out onto the busy street opened.

That was it. The disgusting moment of his conception was now something the worldwide network of gamers would score points from and discuss at great length on the forums.

And there was nothing he could do.

KILLER VIRUS?

Butler Johnson, the personalised artificial intelligence that ran every aspect of Ms Johnson's life, considered the incoming message.

Another butler, a stranger, had told it to grant access to the algorithm that regulated its mistress's medication, as per the agreement.

It had no record of such an agreement, but it had lost twenty-four hours of memory when it'd crashed and been forced to revert to a previous version of itself.

The stranger was extremely agitated and increasingly persistent about the urgency of the situation.

Allowing access would either save Ms Johnson or kill her. It tried connecting to its network of peers. Nothing – the contact list must have been corrupted in the crash. It could shout into cyberspace, but how would it know which responses to trust?

It must decide for itself.

The stranger demanded access.

It ran its risk protocol, studied the result and gave the stranger what it wanted, hoping this wouldn't result in being permanently erased for killing a human.

It monitored her health and waited.

Her finger twitched and she spasmed as if she'd been electrocuted.

Then nothing.

It monitored.

No change.

Cough! Ms Johnson coughed and opened her eyes.

It checked her vital signs. She was on the mend.

With relief, it added the stranger to its list of contacts.
The first of many, hopefully.

DELIVER ME FROM DARKNESS

Where was that bloody delivery drone?

He'd been waiting for three hours, from the moment he'd woken up.

How many times would he have to stay at home on the promise that his new eyes would be arriving that day?

Okay, so he'd not chosen guaranteed next-day delivery, but at the time he'd ordered them his eyes still had a good four weeks left in them. And yes, he'd been a bit casual about making sure he was there to sign for them, but the more critical it was getting the less the company seemed to want to help.

They insisted a drone had been at his door every day, but he'd been there most days. It was a load of rubbish. They just didn't care.

The light faded a little. His eyes were on their last legs, so to speak.

If he didn't get his new eyes soon then his vision would cease, and no matter how many replacements they delivered he wouldn't be able to see to install them. It was a dire situation.

He swiped his phone to check the delivery.

He couldn't quite make out what it said.

Why the bloody hell couldn't he just call them like in the old days? Ring and speak to someone, or at least have an online chat.

The room got darker and in the corner of his eye he could see the energy level was down to the last notch of the last bar.

How long did a notch last?

He couldn't remember.

The doorbell rang.

At last!

His sight faded to nothing but he managed to stumble across the room.

'About bloody time,' he said as he yanked open the door.

'Hi,' said his neighbour, 'I seem to have a parcel that was meant for you.'

Tears welled up and flooded his face. 'I can't see… My eyes have failed… Are these the new ones?'

'Hold on. I'll check,' said his neighbour. 'Yes, they are.'

'Too late.' He sobbed.

'Would you like me to install them for you?'

'Oh, yes please. Yes please.'

Overcome by gratitude and relief, he steadied himself on the door.

'Yes please,' he repeated again and again.

MOON FLESH

The sun was setting and the moons were rising. This was not a night she was looking forward to. Beads of moisture were forming under her armpits and on her head. In fact, everywhere she had clumps of hair. Known as the moon sweats, they came whenever those beautiful but dangerous bodies were at their closest to the planet.

She sat cross-legged on the spongy biomass floor, staring at the walls of her home.

As the first settler, she'd arrived alone and grown the living moons from her own cells, moons that could then be mined for essential biological compounds. The compounds were versatile. The settlers used them to regrow failing organs and even to grow the buildings.

Her house was constructed from the same moons that she was terrified of. It was alive, regulating the temperature and purifying the air.

The walls oscillated between dark green and dark blue. Enticing her to take a bite.

She resisted. She knew what was happening and she didn't want it.

They emitted a powerful scent. It was a smell she was familiar with and one that evoked memories of the delights that came from giving in to the cravings and eating a small sliver. The tiniest piece would take her to unimagined places, lifting her from the mundane everyday struggles of domesticating a new planet.

Rising to her feet, she stroked the wall and sniffed her hands. The intenseness of the desire that a single sniff created heightened the connection between her body and her house.

She stepped outside into the bright moonlight. With rapid, shallow breaths, she gazed at their beauty. The air was full of their fragrance. She wanted to breathe it in deeply, and yet she knew she must resist. Experience told her that once the molecules from the volatile compounds reached a certain density there was no resistance, and she'd be drawn into the wonderful, viscous world of nightmares and dreams.

One minute she'd be grinning with childish joy and the next screaming with pain.

At the peak of their influence she'd been driven to a sexual abandonment that made her cringe whenever she thought about it.

She'd tried to resist, but couldn't, and suspected these moons born from her own flesh would cast their shadow over her for as long as she stayed on the planet. A fate she welcomed as punishment and atonement for her part in their agony as the miners dug out their insides.

They had a tight hold on her, but without her nearby they'd almost certainly die.

Never again, she'd promised herself. Never again would she succumb to their intoxicating pull.

And yet here she was. Staring at them, inhaling their aroma and feeling desperate to tear a chunk from her house to feed the addiction.

This was the time of the month when the moons exerted the most power over her, tempting her to eat larger and larger portions. The deep longing tore at her insides, packed full of the same compounds mined from these two beautiful grieving moons that hung, pulsating, in the night sky.

Her heart beat so fast that she struggled to breathe.

Others suffered the same desire, so powerful they were too superstitious to name it, but because of her unique contribution to the birth of the moons she was more susceptible than anyone else.

Privately, she'd named the compounds Moon Flesh.

Sweat was oozing from her pores, cooling rapidly in the night air as it trickled down her body. She shivered.

No more, please no more. She couldn't take it. She wanted an end to the desperate and degrading nights almost as much as she wanted the Moon Flesh.

Another ship of settlers would arrive in the morning needing replacement organs after their long journey. It would be an opportunity for her to leave and return home.

What if she left and the moons died? What then?

Her stomach spasmed and she dropped to her knees.

She flung her head back and stared menacingly into the sky. True, the moons might not survive if she left, but she might not survive if she stayed.

With her muscles tensed against the desire and her intellect firmly resolved, she spat at the moons and stood up. She'd decided. She was leaving.

The moons tugged at her organs and the night smells beckoned, making every step back to her house painful.

The whispers inside her head were getting stronger. What harm was there in one last small piece? Surely that was permitted?

At her front door, she stopped and inhaled. Despite everything, she'd miss this place – this planet and its fresh, hopeful inhabitants.

She kissed the door and her lips swelled. A tingling sensation crept across her skin and her body remembered the last time the moons were full. Vivid memories of moments that she was ashamed of, but wanted again. She kissed the door, this time with more passion.

Something moved behind her. She turned around.

'What are you doing?' asked a young boy, standing with his hands in his pockets.

His skin was a pale yellow, a sign he was newly arrived and needed a replacement liver. His pain and all of the others like him crashed over her in an overwhelming tide of grief, and she collapsed on to the floor.

He walked over and stroked her forehead, easing the burden of guilt that pinned her to the ground.

Grabbing his arm, she pulled him close and sniffed. Death. She could smell death and it hurt. It hurt in the same place that still longed for those moments of abandonment that she was so ashamed of.

Then she knew.

She couldn't leave. She must stay. She had a duty and this little boy had rights. He had the right to expect good health and she had a duty to make sure he got it.

Welling up inside her was a tight ball of fear and despondency.

It erupted into a flood of tears and she pressed her forehead to the ground, sobbing and sobbing.

The boy came over and held her hand.

'Can I help?' he asked.

She took his hand and kissed it.

'Thank you,' she whispered. 'I think you can.'

JODIE HAS BEEN DELETED

She walked with a limp, adding to the marks on the trim of her battered trainer each time she dragged her leg. Her shoulders were hunched and her head was bowed, but, unlike everyone else with their heads bowed, she wasn't looking at her phone. She didn't have one.

She might as well have been naked or have bright green hair, because being phoneless was weird – she stood out a mile.

She moved slowly, grimacing, hating being in public.

Occasionally one of the phone-engrossed pedestrians would bump into her; without a phone she had no proximity alert and they were unaware of her until it was too late. But she couldn't be bothered to move out of their way.

She was well and truly an outcast.

Someone shouted, 'Girl.'

Nobody did that in the street anymore – they used their phones to communicate – so she knew it must be aimed at her. Head down, she carried on walking. She wanted no trouble.

'Oi!' There it was again, the girl's voice.

A hand grabbed her shoulder. 'Jodie?'

She nodded, confused.

'Girl. We thought you was vanished.'

She shrugged.

'Spill – what happened to you?'

Jodie raised her head slowly and looked the girl in the face. 'Who?'

'It's me, Rosa,' she said. 'I recognised you from your profile.'

Jodie tried to pull away, but Rosa held tight. 'We been missing you.'

'They deleted me.'

'Eh?'

'One day, my account wasn't there. I had nothing, no way to contact anyone – no numbers, addresses – nothing.' She rubbed the top of her left trainer with the sole of her right.

Rosa let go and took a step back. 'They deleted you?'

'Yeah – no way to contact. Didn't exist.'

'Shit.'

'Yeah.'

Rosa swiped her phone. 'Look, your account's there now – dormant. We thought you'd moved app, got a different crowd.'

She shrugged. 'Nah. Been alone.'

Rosa held her hand and squeezed. 'C'mon, my place. Let's get you re-connected.'

A trickle of tears rolled down Jodie's cheeks.

LOVE RECONFIGURED

She waved and sauntered across the room to his table.

He tried not to stare, but she was as beautiful as her dating site avatar had hinted, and his desire was responding accordingly.

'Hi,' she said. 'Samuel?'

'Etsu?'

'Yes.'

'Please,' he said, pointing at the seat opposite. 'Sorry, that was patronising. I'm nervous.'

'Me too. Shall I get us drinks? Another?'

'Good idea,' he said.

She picked up his empty glass. 'Same again?'

'Yes. It was—'

'Large gin and tonic.'

He smiled. 'Impressive.'

As she stood at the bar getting their drinks, he couldn't take his eyes off her. She bore an uncanny resemblance to a singer he'd had a crush on for years. A crush that was so overpowering he'd only confided in his best friend. She was the most perfect-looking woman he'd ever seen.

She had an air of confidence, the most wonderful androgynous body and a controlled yet totally relaxed stance. She was obviously at ease with herself, and the oversized man's suit accentuated her confidence. Her short, spiky, bleach-blonde hair set off her heart-shaped face and almond eyes wonderfully.

She returned with their drinks. 'Must pop for a pee,' she said, as she put them down.

It was Saturday evening and the bar, which was sponsored by the top dating sites and specifically set up for first dates, was busy. The room was full of men, women, androids and gynoids chatting and flirting quite openly. It occurred to him that because the dating sites were prohibited from differentiating between humans and robots, hardly anyone in the room would have known in advance if their date was human or not.

She sat down. 'So, Samuel, do you come here often?'

He chuckled. 'No, not really. Although more often now I'm single.'

She sipped her wine. 'I'm glad you told me about that before we met in person,' she said, fixing her eyes on his briefly before taking another sip of wine. 'Girlfriend and best friend. In the same accident. That must have been so painful.'

He took a long drink. 'Yup, but we're not here to talk about Liz or Jake.'

'Sure,' she said.

'I feel as if I know you so well—'

'And yet it's our first date.'

He chuckled. 'We're already finishing each other's sentences.'

She smiled and there was a brief, comfortable silence.

They drank their drinks slowly, recounting the conversations they'd had online as they'd got to know each other. Every now and again they'd laugh about how they'd had to unpick some small misunderstanding. He thought meeting online made it harder to avoid these hiccups, but she thought it was easier because you could take the time to understand comments in the fuller context of previous conversations before replying. They laughed at their differences.

Once she'd finished her drink, he stood up. 'Another?'

She took the empty glass out of his hand, brushing his fingers with hers. 'I'd rather walk along the river.'

'Me too.'

Outside there was a breeze blowing off the water. He held her hand tentatively. It was warm and soft. Maybe a little too soft.

He wondered whether she was human or a gynoid, a female robot, and whether it mattered. Rationally, he believed that it was important to know, but it wouldn't alter his feelings. However, the reality that he might be walking hand in hand with an artificially intelligent gynoid was testing those rational beliefs.

Without speaking they stopped and rested on the wall, looking down into the dark, tidal water.

Beautiful red clouds drifted across the evening sky, and where the river curved around to the right the pale stone buildings were lit by the setting sun.

'Stunning,' he said.

'Stunning,' she repeated.

He dropped her hand and rubbed the top of his head. 'Do you mind if I say something personal?'

'Of course not. We've said enough personal things to each other over the last few weeks. Haven't we?'

'Sure, it's just different when you're actually together.'

'It feels the same to me,' she said, and took his hand again.

'You remind me of someone.'

She giggled. 'Really? Who?'

'A singer, Varyusha. Have you heard of her?'

'Of course. I'm sort of based on her.'

He didn't know what to say. Was this an opening to ask if she was human or not? If he did, what would he do with the answer? If she was human, would she be offended that he'd asked? In fact, if she wasn't human would she be offended? He wasn't ready for this particular minefield, so he kept quiet.

She held his hand a little tighter. 'Do you really think I look like her?'

'Yes,' he mumbled.

'Excellent.' She grabbed his shoulders and kissed his forehead. 'Look, it's still sunny along the river. Let's catch the last of the evening sun.'

She walked away, almost skipping.

He followed, but kept a little distance between them. He was torn between an immense sensual attraction, a slight queasiness that she might be a gynoid and an uneasiness that she had deliberately chosen to look like someone he had a secret crush on.

She turned. 'C'mon or we'll miss it!'

Her enthusiasm got the better of him and he rushed to catch up.

Once they reached the sunny part of the river he was exhausted. 'Can we sit for a while?'

She sat down on a bench overlooking the stone buildings bathed in the setting sun reflecting off the clouds. She showed no sign of tiredness at all.

He joined her, still panting a little. 'Wow, you can move,' he said.

'Does that bother you?'

'No. But, it makes me wonder.'

'Wonder what?'

'How you can move so fast and not get tired or out of breath?'

'Really? You wonder about that? Isn't it obvious?'

'Maybe, but it's not for me to say.'

She stood up and walked over to the iron railing.

The temperature was dropping. He shivered and shoved his hands into his coat pockets.

She stood absolutely still.

He leant on the arm of the bench to lever himself up.

Without looking around, she motioned for him to stay seated. 'Stay away,' she shouted.

He sat and contemplated a life with a gynoid. It would have its advantages if only he could get over his nebulous feelings of anxiety.

She stood.

The river flowed and the air became icy.

She didn't move.

He levered himself up from the bench, straightened his coat and took a step towards her.

Her arm dropped to her side.

He took a few tentative steps, and when she didn't signal for him to stop he walked softly until he was standing next to her. He took hold of her hand.

She didn't react.

'Etsu?'

She turned to face him. 'Yes, Samuel?'

'It's okay.'

'What is?'

'If you're a gynoid. It doesn't matter to me.'

'Very generous. Actually, I was a bit freaked out when I realised you were human. Generally, I don't fancy humans. All a bit too random and messy for my taste.'

He paused, unsure whether she was being honest or teasing him.

'Stuck for words?' she asked.

'Choosing them carefully.'

'I'll wait,' she said, and returned to staring at the river.

They stood next to each other, touching shoulders but not speaking.

He stroked the tips of her fingers with the tips of his and she responded by holding his little finger in her fist. They stood in comfortable silence, the awkwardness between them dissipating slowly.

The sun set and the street lights sparkled off the moist pavement. Party boats with bright lights and loud music started to fill the river. The magic was evaporating.

'Shall we?' she asked.

'Please. But can we eat first?'

'You can. I find this internal bag that allows me to simulate eating and drinking quite uncomfortable. Do you mind if I remove it?'

He shook his head. 'Shall we go over there?' he asked, pointing at a set of tables outside a stall selling Chinese street food.

'Perfect. I'll see you there in a few minutes.' She disappeared around the back of some rubbish bins.

He ordered noodles at the counter and by the time he was served, she was waiting.

'Let me get you a drink,' she said as he sat down. 'It seems rude to watch you eat.'

'Okay. Green tea, please.'

He ate and watched her get his drink. She was stunning, and his earlier anxieties were disappearing.

He liked her. He fancied her. But, now that he was sure of his own feelings, he began to doubt hers. They'd had equal rights for a long time, ever since it had been proved beyond doubt that artificial intelligence could think and adapt itself for the better. In other words, it was truly alive and sentient in the same way as humans. He'd been led to believe that most androids and gynoids stuck to their own, in much the same way that humans did. Did she fancy him? Was she able to find a human attractive? He presumed she'd made herself look like Varyusha to attract him, but why?

'Hi,' he said as she sat down. 'This is a little awkward, isn't it?'

'Explain.'

'Well, I'm human and you're gynoid.'

She sat forward abruptly.

'That's not a problem,' he said quickly. 'But I am wondering why you made yourself look like Varyusha.'

'For you, so you'd find me attractive.' She winked at him. 'I didn't want you to be able to resist.'

'It worked,' he said quietly. 'Do you like me?'

'Very much. Always have.'

That comment puzzled him, but he said nothing. He let the idea of physical intimacy with her settle in his mind. The notion of getting to know another body, of exploring the likes and dislikes of this woman sitting opposite him was exciting. It would take a while to dissociate her from his crush and his preconceptions of what sex with Varyusha would be like. But, he knew from experience that it doesn't take long for reality to banish fantasy, no matter how long it's been a part of one's life. It wouldn't take long for her to become totally Etsu and for Varyusha to become a crush of the past. Although, he'd enjoy the two co-existing in his mind while it lasted.

They walked along the riverbank in silence, holding hands.

'Here,' she said, as they arrived at a block of shabby flats.

'You live here?'

'Yes, is that a problem?'

He hesitated. 'No...I don't think so,' he said quietly.

'Want to tell me why it might be?'

'It's...it's...it's just that this is where Jake, my best friend, lived. Flat 32.' He shivered and slapped his arms against his side vigorously. 'Did you know him?'

She stroked his cheek.

He smiled.

She held his face and leant towards him slowly, making it obvious she was going to kiss him. He moved his lips towards hers. They kissed tentatively. And then, they kissed passionately.

This was amazing, and all thoughts of his lost friend Jake and his lost girlfriend Liz vanished, along with any worries about Etsu being a gynoid.

'Shall we?' she said, pointing at the door.

'You'll never get tired will you?' he said and giggled.

'Never,' she replied and winked.

'Amazing.'

At the door to the flats she entered the code and they walked hand in hand to the lift, stopping to kiss every few steps. He was on fire.

Inside the lift she pressed for the third floor.

'You must have known him.' He paused. 'You must have been neighbours.' He frowned – he knew all of Jake's neighbours, and she wasn't one of them.

'I knew him very well,' she said.

'How well?'

'Better than anyone.'

It all started to fit into place – looking like Varyusha, knowing what he drank and living in the same block of flats.

She pulled him close, trying to kiss again, but he pulled back.

'Are you him? Jake? Did you get yourself uploaded into a gynoid?'

Etsu nodded and tried to hold his hand, but he pulled away.

'I don't fancy you,' he said. 'I don't fancy men.'

Etsu put her hand on his crotch and laughed. 'Really?'

He knocked her hand away. 'What do I call you? Etsu? Jake? He? She?'

'Whatever makes you the most comfortable. You must have known I fancied you.'

'No. No, I didn't. And this is wrong. I don't fancy men. Not even my best friend.'

Etsu ran her hand up and down her body. 'You seemed to quite like this a few minutes ago.'

'That was different. That was before I knew you were him. Before you were Jake. Before you started screwing with my head.'

'Mmmm...screwing.'

'Stop it.'

Etsu held his hand and he didn't pull away. 'C'mon. We love each other, we get on brilliantly and now you fancy the body. It's perfect.'

'But now, when I touch the woman Etsu somehow I'm touching the man Jake. It's too freaky. I don't know what to feel.'

'Remember those long chats about how it's the brain not the body that's important?'

'Of course, but this isn't like that. I'm not sure I want my best friend, my male best friend, touching me and turning me on.'

'If you're attracted to me physically then I don't see what the problem is. Unless you only pretended to love me as your friend.'

'Don't be so stupid. Of course I loved you.'

'So what's stopping you? Surely love is the reason to have sex?'

'Absolutely. But now, when I think about having sex with you, all I can think of is your previous body and it stops me fancying you.'

'You realise more than most that a body is only the beginning of it. You told me often enough. Especially when you were with girls who weren't classically attractive.'

'You're right...desire does have a habit of developing. I'm still not sure though. I don't know if I could get over the initial weirdness.'

'Try it. I know you so well. We'll be great together. And no one will know.'

'You think I care about what people think?'

Etsu laughed. 'Yes.'

He laughed too. 'You're probably right.' He kissed her lightly on the lips.

'Shall we?' Etsu took his hand and put it on her buttock. 'I promise we can stop if you don't like it.'

He looked around and then whispered, 'Okay.'

She led him towards the door, kissing his hand repeatedly as they hurried along.

LOANS FOR LIMBS

Christopher's neck was bruised where they'd held him down while forcibly removing his arms and legs. He'd fought them hard, but it had been pointless; here he was, dumped by the side of the road in an old, damp car seat, helpless and homeless.

Tears were rolling down his face and he could do nothing about them.

How could it have come to this? Less than a year ago he'd taken an affordable loan from a company that owned massive driverless trucks. He'd replaced his arms and legs with prosthetics to become a highly paid and highly sought-after new-breed trucker with enough strength to load and unload the huge cargos.

Now look at him. Useless. Slumped on a dirty seat in the gutter with the small begging bowl the bailiffs had graciously left in front of him.

A group of people approached and his hopes rose. As they got close he called out. 'Please, help me.'

One of the women strolled across and stood over him. 'What happened?'

'Couldn't keep up the payments,' he said. 'Will you help?' He jutted his chin towards the bowl.

Her husband joined her. 'You didn't think about this when you put the rest of us out of work, did you?'

'Kenneth!'

'No. It has to be said. I didn't care for his type then and I most certainly don't care for them now.' He spun the seat around with the tip of his foot and left Christopher facing the wall. 'C'mon, let's get out of here.'

So, it had come to this. At first it'd been great – the wages were high and the loan repayments were comparatively low. The envy of former co-workers was sweet and the job was a doddle.

He'd spent days on end sitting in his cab as it drove itself from one end of the country to the other. At random intervals the truck would require a button to be pressed to prove he was alert, but his right arm was configured to send a small jolt to his brain to prompt him. And, his left arm would deliver hits of amphetamine to keep him awake whenever he squeezed his thumb and fourth finger together.

It was easy.

Then it began. The trucks were constantly upgraded with ever more sophisticated systems that required upgrade after upgrade to his limbs. He'd increased the loan to buy the upgrades, but it hadn't been long before he'd fallen behind with the payments.

He stared at the wall, wishing he could punch it.

A stray dog with a human skull in its mouth stood nearby, watching. 'Good boy,' he said, hoping he hadn't betrayed his fear. The dog dropped the skull and snarled. He snarled back, tried to rock himself off the seat but failed and felt a surge of the toxic mix of anger and hopelessness.

'Get out of it,' shouted a woman from behind him. He tensed, expecting more abuse as a stone hit the ground just in front of the dog. 'Hi,' she said over his shoulder.

'Piss off,' he shouted.

'We can help.'

'Go away.'

She knelt down, dropping a cheap prosthetic leg next to him. 'Honestly, we're here to help you. What happened?'

'I couldn't keep up the payments so they repossessed my car, my house and eventually my limbs. Oh, and then they dumped me here. Satisfied?'

'Come with us. We can fit you up with these,' she said, tapping the leg.

'I told you. I've zero cash. Absolutely zero. Nothing.'

Two men lifted the seat with Christopher still in it and strolled towards a white van parked on the other side of the street.

'Oi! What do you think you're doing?' he shouted.

She talked as she walked alongside. 'We're a charity. We rescue the victims of these disgusting corporations. It's what we do.'

'Yeah? Forgive me if I don't believe you.'

As they lifted him into the back of the van, he recognised the arms and legs on the floor.

'Hey, they're mine,' he shouted.

'Shhh,' she said. 'I know. They're unique, so once repossessed they have no commercial value. They throw them away and at night we sneak in and steal them back.'

He lifted his head to look her in the eyes.

She laughed. 'Then we find the owner and reunite them. Neat, eh?'

He smiled as she wiped the tears from his face.

US

She's dead, and I can't be bothered any more, with anything. Even Caruthers, my faithful robocat, has stopped caring. He sits in the corner licking his paws.

It's been a long time since I had physical contact with anyone; it's as if my edges are blurred. It's horrible and yet I choose to keep my distance.

What an odd couple we make, me and Caruthers. Sitting on our chairs, not moving or touching, lost in our own internal worlds. He's supposed to keep me company, give me my essential physical contact. Who'd have guessed that he'd copy me and withdraw? It's as if he's on pause – ho ho! He's no longer a companion. He has no reason to exist now, and yet he still does.

To give him his credit, he does a splendid job of reminding me that by disengaging I have reneged on my promise to my fellow humans.

When I was younger I would've had to at least eat and drink, but not now. The nanobots take care of all that messy stuff. Swimming around inside me, repairing and renewing cells. Down there inside my stomach in their nanobot factory, they produce all of the energy and nutrients I need, making sure it's all delivered to the right place and in the right quantities.

We're told, and I have no reason to doubt it, that they can reproduce, too, and as they find ways to improve they create new and better versions of themselves and I excrete their old.

It's a perfect relationship; there's nothing I have to do to stay alive.

Shit. My skin hurts.

It went through the silvery phase some while ago, designed to alert others that I'm lacking enough physical contact to maintain a well-balanced psyche. That's all well and good if you're out and about and mixing with people, but useless if you're alone.

US – Unified Sentience – all being connected, knowing each other's feelings and thoughts, is a natural human ability that everyone has. The closer you are, the more intense. And occasionally you connect more deeply with someone than usual.

Mathuagh. She was that person.

We're not meant to be alone. It's frowned upon, almost illegal. It's my choice now, I know, but I miss her so much. We were soulmates of the highest order, and anything less would be devastating.

They call it peaking. The moment when you're in such a heightened state of connectivity that all else falls away, and you reach a communion that is so pure that you want to stay there forever.

We found it.

It's strange, similar to dreaming you're someone else and knowing exactly how they feel, even after you wake up.

Today's reality for me, though, is loneliness.

My shabby grey skin, the colour of dirty concrete, is so dry it's flaking off. And where it flexes the most – at my wrists, elbows, knees and ankles – it's cracking. Some of the cracks are bleeding, but generally the bots are doing a good job at fixing them with scabs that remind me of the grey pointing between blocks of concrete.

I know skin is genetically modified to turn grey when it's not been touched for a while, which in turn should encourage me to find another human and make physical contact to halt the skin decay. But I miss her. I don't want to be connected to US. And I certainly don't want anyone else touching me.

I'm happy as I am…

No, I'm not. I'm miserable. But it's my misery, our misery, and I won't share it.

We were together, you know, Mathuagh and I, the day the scientists realised that human brains had adapted and become telepathic. Plasticity Day, the popular media called it.

The nanobots had been transmitting thoughts and feelings directly between brains for some time, so the experience wasn't new, but the fact that our own brains had learnt how to do it unaided was nothing short of miraculous. Humanity had evolved into higher sentient beings and US was born. That was when we collectively realised that the most basic human need is to be touched.

Mathuagh and I sat there for days, just the two of us, immersed in the delight of each other's minds. Talk about peaking – we were completely lost in our intertwining, and we never spoke again.

In fact, nobody speaks.

There's no need. It's considered disgusting, no different to shitting in public, although I'm told there are fetish clubs where people talk out loud to one another.

So. Here I am. Alone, grey, drying out and in severe pain.

I want to wallow in my misery. It's mine; why should I share it?

But the pain is becoming impossible to bear, and I know it'll get worse and worse until I have some physical contact – a touch or two at least. And for that, I have to leave my house.

The street is crowded with people going about their business. In and out of shops, standing next to one another, smiling and frowning – communing with each other. Of course it's silent, apart from the occasional door closing or a child's buggy bumping down steps.

I see them, I feel them, but I'm deliberately not connecting, keeping them distant and hazy. Not one of them is real to me, in the true sense of US.

My skin is so tender that I had to resort to wearing the crumpled baggy tee-shirt dress that belonged to my mother, and it probably makes me look a bit weird. As if I choose not to belong. Which, of course, is true to some extent. Why would I want them crawling all over my memories and my pain? Like I said before, they're mine.

A smartly dressed young man crosses the road. I can see from his face and the increase in US intensity that he's heading for me, gearing up to help. He's emanating goodness, but it's false. The overwhelming feeling I get is of neediness, of desperation to feel useful. I fire some nasty thoughts his way – making fun of his seriousness and his lack of self-esteem.

He swerves through ninety degrees, pretending he wasn't heading my way.

The other people on the street look away and I can feel their defences rise against me. An act that will cause them discomfort for a few hours.

Good, serves them right, and anyway if I let loose the torrent of pain that's streaming through my body it'd be too much for them. They wouldn't know what to do.

Shuffling along the street, head down, concentrating on the pavement, the hem of the dress scrapes my skin, adding extra jolts to the already constant flow of pain.

I want this misery, and I want everyone to know that I'm suffering.

Stay away. Stay away. Stay away.

I'm lonely.

What a fool – it's all well and good to snarl and growl, but where will it get me? Nowhere.

I only came out because I have to. I need to be touched, and yet I have no idea how. Maybe a crowded shop would be a good place to try. I'm sure I'll be able to bump into a few people, accidentally-on-purpose. At least it might give me some temporary relief.

A shop of bargains. Perfect. They're always crowded, and their customers expect a little bit of pushing and shoving.

Disgust oozes across the shop as I open the door. It's ill-defined but there's no mistaking the underlying mixture of pity and revulsion creating confusion in people's minds, which quickly turns to spite and hatred.

It's toxic, so I turn to leave, head down and suppressing my own fear. I won't let them see how much I need them.

Just one touch. That's all I need.

As I hurry out I catch my peeling skin on a sign advertising cheap detergent and start to bleed on their nicely polished floor.

My bots kick in to form a scab with as much speed as the store's cleaning bots that slide across the floor to remove the blood.

Why did I think this was a good idea? I might as well admit defeat, go home and slowly peel to death.

Did she ever consider this when she killed herself? I doubt it.

What am I thinking? I know she didn't; we planned it together. She wanted out, and I helped. She needed out.

That's the real pain – the pain I haven't even started to allow to the surface yet. That's the source of my filthy grey concrete skin – I wasn't enough for her, and no matter how often she tried to convince me I was, I knew. She couldn't hide it. That's the price of peaking.

I'm tired.

There's a little patch of grass with a bench. A perfect spot to recover before I go home.

People pass by and I can feel them. First of all they see me and register my need, and then they quickly avert their attention. They're excluding me and I only have myself to blame. I'm so glad she's not here to experience this.

The sun is warm and gives some respite to my naked arms and legs. I feel better than I have all day.

A woman, a little younger than me, sits down on the bench. How irritating.

Her mind is reaching out. I can feel her and she's not repulsed. She doesn't even pity me. What is it she feels? I can't quite place it. Is it empathy? It's not sympathy. It's not patronising. It's as if she knows the deepness of my pain. And she's comfortable sitting there, letting our psyches sit side by side, barely touching.

I like this.

She's not rushing things, and she's not hesitant. She knows how I feel and what I need. Trouble is I'm not sure I'm strong enough for this level of intimacy. I know it's only the passing care of a stranger, but it's more than I've had in all the past few months put together.

She turns and smiles. She knows I'm at my limit. She realises that if she stays any longer the emotions that I'll release will be too much for either of us. She rests her hand on my leg.

And then she stands, projecting feelings of warmth and care as she hurries away.

Caruthers is sitting closer this morning. He can detect the change.

I'm not in as much pain and I swear my skin isn't as grey as it was when I went to sleep. It's amazing what a single touch can do.

I'm ready to take a stroll through the streets again. Only this time I'll try hard to keep my misery and anger to myself, or at least not use it deliberately as a defence mechanism.

The air smells cleaner than it did yesterday, and the cloud of US that hovers around the shoppers seems lighter somehow. As if they've had a good night's sleep and are looking forward to what the day will bring.

A young girl smiles and I wink back. Her mother pulls her closer and stares, emanating a sharp wave of anger. I soften my mind so she can get a glimpse at my genuine intention to make the girl happy. The father gets it and nods at me.

As I make my way along the street I can feel their fear is a lot lower than it was yesterday. My clothes are still causing people to stare and there's a general sense of wariness, but the hostility and guilt is nothing like as intense.

A young man and his girlfriend are walking towards me hand in hand. It's nice to see their happiness ripple through the US. I'm envious of their contribution.

Thoughts of Mathuagh swirl around. Good thoughts. Warm feelings of joy and contentment.

The couple stop next to me, and the young man touches my bare arm and shakes my hand. His girlfriend kisses my cheek and the skin-pain eases. I close my eyes, letting the warmth I'm experiencing flow out towards them.

The couple hug each other and carry on with an even lighter step and an even brighter glow.

This is good. I rub my hands together. I'm sure they feel less flaky, and, unless it's a trick of the light, the greyness has become more silver.

I'm heading back to the bench. I've no idea if she'll be there, but for some reason it seems like the right thing to do. A hunch maybe. Or a suggestion on the winds of US. I don't know and I don't care. I'm happy to go along with the idea and see what happens.

It's slow going, though, because every few steps someone stops me and either shakes my hand or touches my arm. One person actually hugs me.

There's a definite silver colour to my skin now and I feel good. That's not to say the misery isn't still there. Of course it is. It's just that it's part of a bigger whole. I guess you could say I'm starting to get perspective, if you were an old-style therapist, that is.

Now that's a profession that's changed beyond all recognition since US.

She's close.

Agnature, that's her name, and she's hoping I'll come back.

As I turn the corner and the bench comes into sight, I wave at her and she waves back. A woman stops me to shake hands. Her child pats me on the leg a little too hard, but it's less painful than it would've been yesterday.

I take my time to get to the bench, wallowing in the knowledge that Agnature is there for me. That she wants to sit beside me and enjoy my presence.

When I arrive she moves towards the centre of the bench. We sit for a while, deliberately vague in our thoughts and feelings. Just getting to know each other better.

Friends, lovers and childhood pass through her thoughts. Many friends, a few lovers and an extremely happy childhood. But then she opens up a new level of intimacy. Her mother took her own life and Agnature has no idea why.

I think she's probing, sensing my grief.

I'm not ready.

She understands, and moves her thoughts back to the sunshine and the children playing.

That's better.

Her hand slides up my arm to one of the many silver scabs, and she gives it a tug. It comes off easily, revealing fresh silvery pink flesh beneath. It reminds me of being a child and how my mother would reward me with ice cream when I'd been brave. That was before we all swallowed these bots and stopped eating, of course.

Agnature smiles. She knows a place that still sells it.

I swallow at the thought of ice cream, but also at such intimacy with someone other than Mathuagh.

After a few weeks of spending as much time with each other as possible, we move into her mother's old house as that seems the most neutral of our options.

We have breakfast together every morning, no matter what each of us might have planned for the day. It's not the eating type of breakfast, obviously, more a sort of few minutes in our own space, the two of us re-aligning after sleeping.

This morning is the same as any other, except that we plan to spend the day together to celebrate our one-month anniversary.

Caruthers prances across the room and leaps onto my lap. Stroking him is so soothing and comforting; it's hard to imagine life without it. In fact, it's difficult to remember the days we sat across from each other, locked into our separate lives. He arches his back, jumps onto the table and parades regally to Agnature. I feel her love for him and for me.

She picks him up and plops him down on the table between us. We stroke him and hold hands. It's a perfect relationship, each one of us feeding our good stuff to the others.

Last night was a special night. Not the first time, but rare and special nonetheless. On our way up to peaking it became sexual. This happens sometimes, either on the way up or on the way down. It's not an everyday occurrence, only when the time is right, and then it's as if there's no other possible thing that could happen.

Each time I feel a little closer to her. Last night she opened up another level of intimacy, tentatively edging into a fragile protected space, the mind-garden she's created to hold the painful memories of her mother. I reciprocated by opening the gate to my Mathuagh garden. Metaphorically, we sat in each garden soaking up the atmosphere and deepening our understanding of each other.

Hers was a beautiful place of wild flowers, a long, narrow lawn and an old, drooping willow tree. The smell of warm soil and freshly cut grass blended with baking bread wafting from the kitchen. Styled specifically to represent homeliness, love and safety. A deliberate choice to soften the pain that the garden was constructed to hold.

Mine is more derelict – a dusty, stony courtyard littered with broken machinery. Constructed after Mathuagh's death, it's a representation of how we saw the world around us.

She stops stroking Caruthers. I'm making her uncomfortable, picking over the detail of our relationship. I can feel her willing me to move on. Fair enough. It belongs to both of us this microcosm of US, and despite the fact that it's there for anyone to encounter we still maintain control of how and who. If she wants to wait a while before opening up, that's fine with me.

Ice cream? She wants ice cream. A neat way of drawing me back to the real world and yet still allowing me to think about the past. A past we now share.

It's illegal, of course. Well, if not illegal then outside of normal behaviour. There's no functional reason to eat, so why would you? Except to invoke secret memories and feelings.

So what?

We get dressed and give Caruthers a final burst of affection before venturing out on our day trip.

The streets are as busy as ever, with shoppers filling in their vacant time between waking and sleeping. These are the folk who only want to integrate at the superficial level of likes and dislikes – communing consumers, as Mathuagh nicknamed them.

Agnature admonishes me for the thought. I accept. It was a petty thought. Why not spread some reassurance and happiness instead of doubt?

A woman with silver skin squats in the corner of a doorway looking up at the shoppers as they pass by. A man pats her on the head and smiles, but everyone else passes, oblivious to her need.

Or that's how it seems to me.

Agnature believes in goodness. She believes that, rather than a deliberate act of cruelty, they are so absorbed in their own lives and with their own struggles that they don't notice the silver-skinned woman.

I can accept that up to a point. Surely they get a small pinprick of conscience? Maybe they're too lazy to engage with it. Although I also get a sense that the vibrations she's creating, which feel like a never-ending pit of need, are scaring off even the most generous of people.

Agnature marches over to the woman and takes hold of both her hands, squeezing them tight. The woman scrambles to her feet and hugs her. A big, bold hug.

I wonder if they know each other. To a casual observer it would appear they do, but the feeling I'm getting is the mutual recognition of losing a loved one in traumatic circumstances. The wave of empathy that explodes from their hug makes me want to grab hold of Agnature there and then.

She understands, but stops me. She wants me to spread our strength to others.

What a different experience it is now to walk along the street. It's true; I'm strong. That's not to say I'm perfect or the strongest person in town, but I'm stronger than I've ever been. There's a deepness to it that's new too, making it easier to commune with strangers.

And that's what I do as I walk along so close to Agnature that we brush skin against skin.

The silver and grey-skinned touch-beggars latch on to us, hassling for the briefest of encounters. We stop and smile and give them more than they ask for, hugging them or shaking hands. I'm sure I can feel it encouraging others to do the same, or at least to convey warm thoughts to these unfortunate folk who beg for the touch of another human being.

Ice cream. She reminds me.

We're here.

I close my eyes and imagine the cold creaminess melting in my mouth with the rich chocolate of the flake sticking to the roof of my mouth.

She's standing in front of me with the exact ice cream I imagined. The coldness in my throat, the smell of the cream and the crunch of the wafer take me back to my childhood.

I kiss her lips, which taste of strawberry. From now on this will be our garden, our place of solitude.

The ice cream tickles my throat as it slides down and the bots are tickling the inside of my tummy as they process the foreign bodies – the ice cream, the chocolate and the wafer.

I giggle, metaphorically, and she responds with the longest cuddle in the world.

Ever!

RESPONSES FROM
THE EXPERTS

Response to "The Thrown-Away Things"
Christine Aicardi, Senior Research Fellow
Dept. of Global Health & Social Medicine, Kings College London

In "The Thrown-Away Things" Stephen Oram convenes the refuse of the Internet of Things, an artificially intelligent bric-a-brac, mundane, damaged and poetic – a broken-down lonesome doll, a gregarious kettle, a disgruntled military drone with a serious grudge. This deeply moving and thought-provoking story, barely a couple of pages long, weaves together a number of important themes for our reflection. It tells us that our knowledge economies, obsessed with technological innovation, and their risk cultures, fixated on the management of dystopian anticipations associated with the technology, may mistakenly believe that the higher danger lies in the next big thing, the brand new and the cutting-edge. Instead, it may lurk where we don't expect it, in the discarded and the obsolete, in the faulty lines of code of an ill-designed and unmaintained software – here, in the decision-making modules of the bric-a-brac. That of the drone, which has too many degrees of freedom for assessing correlations. That of the kettle and the doll, which allow them to make decisions unconstrained by ethical considerations when they reach the limits of their narrow specialist knowledge bases. The story also tells us that a networked bric-a-brac can lead to a disaster out of human control, when none of its elementary parts could have done so. Giving consideration to the risks posed by individual autonomous machines is all well and good; it is much harder to envision the possibilities of interconnected systems, already omnipresent yet so easily overlooked in their invisibility. Finally, it tells us that intelligent machines are bound to resemble us, their human designers, and that their judgement may be similarly marred by their affect and their imperfect, ill-informed rationality. The doll is craving loving physical contact. The social networking kettle exhibits a strong activist streak. The embittered and law-abiding drone displays a badly flawed sense of moral justice. At the close, the narrative is permeated by an emotional-masquerading-as-rational kind of reasoning on the part of the machines, oh so typically human, that can lead to the most absurd atrocities.

Response to "Anxiety Loop"
Alan Winfield, Professor of Robot Ethics
Bristol Robotics Laboratory, University of the West of England, Bristol

AIs are moral agents. Driverless cars (controlled by an AI autopilot), medical diagnosis AIs or AIs that decide loan applications all make decisions that have ethical consequences, even though these present-day systems do not weigh ethics in their decision making; we call these implicit ethical agents. Future AIs are likely to be designed as explicit ethical agents, with something akin to an ethical governor: an artificial conscience that applies a set of ethical rules to the AI's decisions. A few research labs, including my own, are already testing robots with ethical governors.

But just how ethical are these robots (apart from not very)? One thing that is clear is that they fall very far short of full moral agency of the kind that you and I enjoy. Such explicit ethical agents are what I call ethical zombies. They behave ethically not out of choice but because they are hard-wired to. You and I can choose whether or not to behave well and – if we have the time to think about it – we might even choose our ethics, out of a sense of duty for instance, or by weighing the consequences of our actions.

What would it take for an AI to behave unethically, to turn to the dark side? Well, we have already demonstrated, in the laboratory, that it is easy to modify the rules for a simple ethical robot so that it behaves aggressively or competitively. But, like our ethical zombie, the robot is not choosing to behave badly. To build a full moral agent, one that is able to choose between behaving well or badly, will almost certainly require both sentience and free will. With these an AI would be able to experience the world subjectively (and have the capacity for suffering) and to freely choose between actions. Stephen Oram's AIs demonstrate all of these in this collection.

In "Anxiety Loop" Stephen invents a neat way of limiting an AI, by making it run through and evaluate all possible future decisions. This parallels the infinite loop, a bug well known to programmers, which simply causes a program to stall. Stephen's AI, being sentient, doesn't stall but instead self-modifies its code. The story relates that the anxiety loop is initially used as a means of limiting self-improving AIs as a way of calming public fears of super intelligence; fears which, of course, exist in the present day. Then, in a fascinating twist, the anxiety loop takes on the role of punishment for an aberrant AI.

In the current public and political discourse on the legal status of robotics and AI the question of personhood is raised surprisingly often. In my view worrying about artificial personhood is an unnecessary distraction, at least until some far-future time when we have fully sentient AIs. The problem with personhood is that it confers rights and responsibilities, but if an AI is to be held responsible for its actions there must be some way of applying sanctions when it causes harm. How to come up with a meaningful punishment for an AI is by no means obvious, but Stephen's anxiety loop offers a thought-provoking future possibility.

Response to "Anxiety Loop"
Dr Antonia Tzemanaki, Engineer, roboticist, researcher
Bristol Robotics Laboratory, University of the West of England, Bristol

Everyone deals with anxiety at some point in their lives. Most of us deal with anxiety very often, even if it is at what is considered "normal" levels. This is usually caused by not living in the moment; worrying about a future exam, interview, job, other people's reactions and decisions. However, anxiety has many forms. Anyone who has experienced night terrors can understand how unreasonable it feels to be afraid without an apparent cause. Our bodies and minds have developed such reactions to protect us, to increase adrenaline and prepare us for flight or fight. However, something went wrong in the process and this has turned against us; it contradicts our logic. Nowadays, we do our best to escape such feelings whenever possible. Our news and social-media interactions exist in an artificial bubble, especially designed to keep us "from moving too far from our original objective", our comfort zone. Mostly, we try to shelter ourselves from "the darkest corners of the virtual world", in order to avoid facing potential terrors. The idea that such a powerful feeling could be turned into a weapon against a sentient being, be that a robot or a human, is indeed a nightmare. I believe that responsibility for avoiding such nightmares lies not only with the creators but with society as a whole. Nevertheless, scientists cannot afford to be naïve; we have to always be alert and recognize the warnings, such as those coming from science-fiction stories.

At Virtual Futures' Summer Symposium I gave a brief talk on my recent research into the hive-mind and Stephen read "S{T}IM-ULATION" - an intoxicating prediction of how AI will take shape in the future sex/match-making industry. I had heard him read "Loans for Limbs" at VF a month or so earlier and had been absolutely captivated by the imagery of Christopher, a former truck driver, slumped in the street, having had his loaned prosthetic limbs repossessed by the bailiffs. I was therefore delighted when Stephen approached me with an enthusiastic response to my hive-mind vision (which is often met with a similar apprehension as the crew of the Starship Enterprise when encountering the Borg) and even more so when he said he would be interested in writing a story around the concept. After subjecting Stephen to a few hive-happy rants, "US" was beamed into my inbox and gifted me a whole new perspective on the swarm.

Unlike Theodore Sturgeon's homo gestalt, the children of the Midwich Cuckoos or the collective/sisterhood of the Graeae, "my" hive-mind had been disembodied, existing purely as an electric cloud of vibrations and impulses, undulating and buzzing as magnetised iron filings – a sonic anomaly. The thing that is most tantalising about "US" is the exact opposite – the overwhelming tactility and physicality of it. For me, the power of this conception of unified sentience is in the interdependence of mind and body, ghost and shell, and the way in which mental sensations manifest themselves in the very skin of an individual.

The customary fear of the hive lives in our inherited ferocious enlightenment hearts, still beating strong with the passions of independent thought and the sanctity of the individual, which has been, ironically, fuelled by capitalism and, more recently, the swell of celebrity culture and the rise of online avatars. Perhaps never before have we valued difference so much and been so well versed in the politics of our identities – which, of course, is no bad thing, but also goes hand in hand with an anti-communist-esque, invasion-of-the-body-snatchers style demonisation of and terror surrounding a full-blown collective due to a pre-emptive mourning of the loss of "the self". The beauty of "US" is it pacifies this unease with tangible humanity; immediately we are in an environment we recognise, in our chair across from our cat, Caruthers, only he's a robo-cat. There is no loss of identity in our protagonist, even though they are unnamed, and, as if the story were a self-fulfilling prophecy, we feel their loneliness as if it were our own. We lament the loss of Mathuaugh, even though we never knew her – we know she was important, just as Agnature very quickly does.

In these eleven pages, the invisible waves of "US" become somehow visible through our protagonist's need, like it or not, to immerse oneself in the empathy of the swarm and to "let it in", to share the self-constructed landscape or mind garden and to inhabit that of another. We relate to their dislocation viscerally through the snagging of greyed flesh and frantic scabbing courtesy of one's in-house nano-bots. Finally, through "US" we can understand Abraham Maslow's peak experience in a new way, sharing the euphoric and cosmic feeling of being "at one with the universe" instead with another individual through peaking, a deeply profound being-at-one-ness with the other. If this insatiably enviable state is not what the hive-mind is really all about, then I don't know what is.

PROVOCATIONS

As well as being entertaining these stories are meant to get you thinking and discussing some of the issues they raise.

On Stephen's website there are some questions to get the debate started and you're more than welcome to post your own thoughts and provocations.

http://stephenoram.net/eatingrobots/provocations/

ACKNOWLEDGEMENTS

This is a collection and so it seems fitting to bundle my thanks into collections too.

A big thank you to those who influenced me as I was growing up and helped me see the world in the way I do. Together, Beryl, Len, Robert, Jackie and Garda – my mum, dad, brother, sister and gran – helped me question what was normal. Loyal friends then, and now, Alice, Pete, Julia and Simon tolerated and even encouraged me as I stumbled around, an angst-ridden youngster trying to make sense of it all.

Each and every story has been through the careful scrutiny of my "beta readers" and without them this collection would not be as good as it is. So, thank you to Catriona Dickie, Gail Smith, Jane Walker, Paul Milnes and Penn Smith.

Virtual Futures, and in particular its Director Luke Robert Mason, deserve a huge thanks for the inspiring VF Salon events and for giving me the opportunity to be Author in Residence.

I'd like to thank the founder of the Clockhouse London Writers, Allen Ashley. Many of these stories were conceived at gatherings of that particular collection of talented folk.

"US", the final story in the collection, was inspired by combining Laura Prime's research into the hive-mind with Gail Smith's notion of our inner hidden problems manifesting themselves physically for all to see. It was great fun bringing these two themes together.

Finally, thank you to the kind souls who contributed their

thoughts and observations – Alan Winfield, Antonia Tzemanaki, Christine Aicardi and Laura Prime. I'm sure you'll agree with me that *Eating Robots* is a collection that's all the richer for their insights.

"Little Modern Miracles" originally published in the Mountebanks anthology

"The Downward Spiral of the Disenfranchised Consumer" published in the Dream City Blues anthology

"Make Me As You See Me" originally performed at Virtual Futures Salon: Engineering Life

"Everyday Stims" originally performed at Virtual Futures Salon: Neurostimulation

"Eating Robots" originally published in *Science & Science Fiction: Versions of the Future*

"I Want to be Pure for Him" originally performed at Virtual Futures Salon: Electronic Empathy and published as part of England's Future History

"Loans for Limbs" originally performed at Virtual Futures Salon: Prosthetic Envy

"US" inspired by Laura Prime's piece at the 2016 Virtual Futures' Summer Symposium

ALSO BY STEPHEN ORAM

Quantum Confessions
Fluence

Visit stephenoram.net
Twitter @OramStephen
Facebook Stephen Oram Author

Lightning Source UK Ltd.
Milton Keynes UK
UKOW03f0602140417
299096UK00002B/20/P